Journey of the Internal Dermis

SAMUEL HATHY

authorHOUSE®

AuthorHouse™
1663 Liberty Drive
Bloomington, IN 47403
www.authorhouse.com
Phone: 1-800-839-8640

Published by AuthorHouse 11/11/2014

ISBN: 978-1-4969-5289-9 (sc)
ISBN: 978-1-4969-5288-2 (e)

Contents

INTRODUCTION

This novel is a one about self-discovery. I was driven to write it after a weekend that changed my life. What put the so to speak icing on the cake was a book by Jack Kerouac which was the best thing I could have read around the time. It is a sort of thank you to some of the people that played a role in changing my life. I don't know it sounds a bit sentimental; I just hope it is enjoyed by others I guess. The persons in this novel are entirely fictitious or at least partially false anyway; in other words they were based on real people but are given different names and while most of the situations are based on real life I might add a few details, I might not who knows. Any exaggerations are completely coincidental if you know you are in this book I apologize if you feel uncomfortable with your character as I said before any exaggerations are coincidental and reflect my feelings as the music I listened to as I write shapes my emotions as I look back on these events I remember with great fondness even the not so great moments I remember with fondness. I apologize if you don't like my writing but I don't really give a shit. It is a mix of rant, with attempted poetic prose at moments, mostly improvisational remembrance and a bit of knowledge I have acquired from other books and thinkers to shape my feeling about the situations. It is a work of art and it is not artistic at all. It is largely autobiographical but trying break the mold.

"Prison is somewhere you promise yourself
the right to live" – Jack Kerouac

CHAPTER 1

The Christian Fool

There was a man that walked over to me some days ago. I have no idea who this man was or even his name. He seemed to know me though I remember seeing him some other time at the college. He said, "Hey aren't you Geoffrey's son" when I replied that I was he continued to blabber on about it and how we went to the same church. I never seen him in my life but I was polite to him I shook my head and everything when he spoke and acted like I was paying attention which I guess I was but only in part like I could remember everything he said it wasn't interesting enough to repeat and it's nothing you didn't already know from reading the previous scripting.

I could probably say I remembered seeing him three times in my whole life. The first time I mentioned in some detail the second he didn't speak more than a sentence. I happened to bump into the man when coming to see a college speaker talking about a situation between Russia, Crimea and the Ukraine. It was allot of trouble and nothing I didn't really know but I can never remember the specific details about things like that. It doesn't take much time to realize which side was wrong. That is just the thing they were both wrong the Ukrainians some of the resistance to the Russian state were neo Nazis but the Russians were no worse

1

I guess I supported Ukraine more due to the fact Ukraine wasn't invading Russia and Ukraine mostly was riled up and acting in self-defense or so that was how it seemed. I wasn't like there to see it and besides not all Ukrainians were the anti- communist fascists some were probably collective anarchists or something of that nature which is something that I enjoyed thinking about. I liked reading books about it and all that. I read things by brilliant minds like Noam Chomsky, Karl Marx, Howard Zinn, and George Orwell people like that. Anyway getting back to the church man who went to the same college and church but I hadn't been to church in quite a while. I don't think the man knew really but he seemed to like that I was in college learning all these things and whatnot. I was really into philosophy, politics and sociology and the great thing about these studies is that they could all blend into each other. I liked to think I was intelligent but I felt dumb allot of the time. My folks always said I didn't know things because I couldn't see it, I couldn't experience it, I mean I label myself an empiricist but I think that these intellectuals must be mostly right at least. Damn, I am keep going of the topic of this man that saw me at school, probably because he was so uninteresting. The man seemed so proud though of me but he didn't know me, he seemed nice enough but something about him reminded me of one of the Koch brothers, I don't know which one David or Charles there was something I didn't trust about him is what I suppose I am trying to get across and if he only knew what I was reading, if he only knew what I did on the weekend I had yesterday he wouldn't be so proud.

I wouldn't let some religious phony speak about my ignorance. Yes, I am mostly ignorant of the world but I think everyone should admit their ignorance sometimes. That is the problem about how philosophy seemed you were trying to learn all you could but you couldn't say you knew things and that made you seem dumb to people or perhaps others would think you were so smart because when you talked it was always about something of an interesting nature that most can't relate too and you didn't make friends that way. I was really like in the middle; I was always in the middle of everything. I was born in like a middle class family, not abused but perhaps depends on one's perspective of it. I always felt dumb by my friends or certain friends; in comparison they seemed just so smart. It was maybe because I didn't say all that much. I said allot more since after the trip ah, that wonderful weekend when I went to a human rights conference. I don't feel that the old Christian man would like hearing about that. It is not necessarily because he was Christian, he seemed like the typical American Christian, the one that just acts nice but supports the most horrendous policies in politics it seems in the American government. For some reason the more liberal people more, the more terrible people they were when labeled by the media, they were these eccentric crazy people. I don't understand what is crazy or eccentric about being decent. I don't know why I assumed the man was a conservative I don't know why perhaps because he reminded me of the Koch brothers. They were libertarians apparently but they wanted to get rid of public schooling, take people's rights for healthcare and get rid of the ideas of green energy which would force people to live in a dangerous world of unsafe policies on energy; that doesn't sound like liberation it sounds like slavery and oppression of human rights if anything.

Well anyway I suppose I shouldn't judge a book by its cover but I know the man is a Christian. This ideology ruined my life. It limited me from experience and even when I abandoned Jesus and the Lord and all that the church still haunted me like an unwelcome visitor. The Holy Ghost was in my brain and it scared me from everything. It was all sin I tried to deny certain things from entering my mind. They say homosexuality is a sin and I wondered if I was really heterosexual for a time but I discovered that was most likely a falsity, I mean some girls were just well to put it short really attractive. I don't think that I was like most other young men though, I could manage myself and function my brain in the presence of women I wasn't an asshole misogynic bastard that howled like a wolf like in an old cartoon character at a construction site. Then again I wasn't brought up to act in such a way I was raised to think women should not be associated with until I was like the right age or some shit because young brains are too confused and then at a certain point in time I would have the liberty of being a misogynic ass. That never happened and I don't know whether it was my experience of reading feminist literature and resisting an oppressive male over woman relationship but I never was taught how to pursue one from the an egalitarian perspective because that wasn't what the culture expected, it was so engrained even the women were willing to subject themselves to others because society conditions them to get ahead that way. It wasn't easy to find a woman that liked that dynamic. Mostly where I lived was a place where women just wanted to be at home or have jobs that made almost no pay but they felt that was their place and they were fucking wrong, they can do better.

I then attempted to base my opinions on looks and simply how nice they were and stuff but I didn't take any time to know anyone; I would just occasionally glare and I glared at everyone not just women but men too to make sure that I wasn't a sicko and also to see if I liked the looks of some men. The men gave these stares like is this queer checking me out and the women replaced queer or fag with the word pig or misogynic with stares. I continued this anti-social behavior hoping people would feel bad and comfort me or talk even perhaps. I liked talking to people when they were the right people I didn't think I was shy but just real confused and believed all relations must be this overbearing commitment somehow. When I talked to girls and hung around them my father made me feel like an ass and asked if she was my girlfriend and wanted me to pursue that kind of relationship with any girl I met. It made me real paranoid and insecure with myself. My mother was similar about it but real corny like she was trying to act serious about it but it seemed so fake like she was almost making fun of perhaps my attempt to think an engagement with someone else could happen. I had "friends" but I didn't feel too comfortable talking to these people on matters. I felt like a woman almost hoping to be what society expects of women to have people oogle over me instead of me expecting to do that to the opposite gender but was I more a women inside? It felt like it but this was a problem because I assumed sex changes were too expensive which I later found were rather expensive and no one would assist in paying because my parents wouldn't even pay a quarter for a vehicle that I would wish to buy and certainly wouldn't support me being a transsexual. I felt alone and damned to a world of loneliness and I had to accept being an asexual and I didn't want to live without sex no matter how much I would scream I didn't care in my head I wanted to have a deep personal relationship with another woman that involved sexual activity.

Girls seemed to from what I assumed wanted to at one point or another have sex with their men and what not but I would be content with communication, love, and kissing or hugging but no sex would have to happen I would be gay or something if I didn't want it at some time and there would be heart break and embarrassment and I didn't want to risk it, I was too afraid of judgment. I understood women when they were smothered by asshole men and the women said "No" I would hear so many men complain about this and it pissed me off to no end because the ass was upset with even having any kind of care from somebody. I never had care at all and never wanted any. My parents wanted me finding it but I had no idea how and I couldn't just speak to them about it they were so corny so fake so misogynic so Christian so evil. I began to hate the fears that Christianity would instill in me and it was hard to escape despite my abandoning of it like I said before it followed me like a ghost. No escape, no exit, I was a product of my environment and it was so diverse and mixed. My brain was incapable of interpreting it all.

Back to this man that means nothing to me. He was a Christian, knew my dad, went to my church I no longer associated with, never saw him aside from these meeting never talked to him but he seemed to want me to have mutual engagement. He wanted to be my friend. I just said hey and yeah and nodded my head and shit. Saw him twice before the trip and once after. Yes, the trip the one he wouldn't agree with on various levels. He would have not liked my choices on that weekend. He would have been nervous that male and female students were sharing rooms. He would hate that it was upon the business of my school group and larger organization of Amnesty International because some of their goals called for freedom of choice for women and equal rights for the LGBT community and I doubt the man in his environment was inherently enjoyed the company of people who weren't WASPs, and I also got really drunk and he would say how rowdy, how irresponsible. He would judge my opinions if he got to know me we would most likely ending up despising each other perhaps but he didn't know me and I didn't know him.

To me he was just a Christian fool something that would be better if it hadn't exist. People like him were neutering the minds of children killing their experiences and part of their lives. It was a lobotomy of the soul rather than the saving of it. The trip however, this weekend, that most Christian fool would persecute as the people back in the past with the stones smashing against prostitute's heads or witches burnt at the stake. It would be in secret but we would feel the punishment all the same like gossiping girls in a high school. It happened so often it became a stereotype such as that and I knew some Christians were fine as people but I have a deep prejudice towards them. I thought deep in my heart I am transgender and I am proud, I look like a man but wish to science I could be a woman but could love a woman and pursue a lesbian relationship from thenceforth. They hated me and I hated them and that is how it would work deep inside because if I was out loud about such things among the American Christian populace I would be stoned just like the prostitutes. They are all Christians just a bunch of Christian fools.

CHAPTER 2

The Trip

Excuse the jumping around but I am going further into the past; the past preceding the trip that me and my friends were going on. Same place, different time different people, different location. I was at the college not in the library where I met the man before and after my trip. It started here my comrades, my friends, real friends that were interested in things or at least wanted to pretend to be. It was neat thing we went a floor above in one of the student offices and discussed which human rights activities we would do for Amnesty International. We had activities to call attention to certain issues like women's rights, government spying, Guantanamo bay, political prisoners and stuff of that nature. We had people sign petitions, write letters to ensure there may be some justice done and some accountability put on the government which didn't care for anyone at all and that is obvious, everyone knows this. That is not what this is all about, this is about the trip.

Now I have been on an Amnesty Conference trip before and it was loads of fun and we signed more petitions and went to panels where they talked about more things we were all concerned about. My friends were all great and real people like they didn't seem to hide themselves like I did. I hid away but could expose myself occasionally when people were hip or cool. Smart people were cool and dumb people were not that was mostly how things were. I could also talk to dumb people that didn't think they were real smart at least then they didn't know they were so dumb. I liked older people, well, older liberal people. Most old folks seemed like liberals despite popular opinion or belief. You could usually scout them out pretty easily. The old grouchy men and women were conservative when they were happy they were usually otherwise.

The first trip was in Cincinnati, OH and ok but Ohio is such a bland state. The people there were mostly boring. Most groups didn't come from Ohio like rock groups and things. Many were from places like New York, Washington, California and Florida. There was nothing in Ohio. Grunge started in Seattle. Artsy rock came from New York and so did allot of early punk rock. Against Me were from Florida. Bad Religion was from California. Velvet Underground and the Ramones from New York. Dave Grohl had to get out of Ohio to become famous all the way into Washington. I couldn't go anywhere without help, no license, didn't live close to friends with vehicles. I was in the middle of nowhere. I liked school it was a place to get away from the damn country. I hated the country lots of stupid people. They didn't like good music and their politics just as bad. They didn't like homosexuals or lesbians. Colored people were the butt of jokes. A minority of kids tried acting black and that was embarrassing to watch. They just listened to rap and thought that made them similar or like they could somehow understand. I don't think they thought so far into it. The people in college were more like me in high school, they minded their own business most of the time and weren't so loud, and several were intelligent. I had more school work though and was reading a whole lot of shit so I couldn't talk much even though it would have been ok to talk to most of the colleagues.

This trip was to Chicago though. I didn't know what it was like I think we based through it once to see my father's brother in Illinois. That was ok but it wasn't Chicago. I was excited thinking about it due to the fact Rise Against, a band I like was from there. I don't know why this excited me. Anyway, on our way there I recollect someone saying Chicago was like a whole separate place than the rest of Illinois. That was pretty accurate because it was rather different. I don't remember my first trip there being nearly as entertaining. I liked cities. My parents didn't they drove in them anxiously waiting to escape. My dad was a truck driver so he spent some time there and could navigate through it but it was more complicated and he didn't like it. He was a simple man with simple needs and simple wants. That I liked about him allot of people want so much out of life and pursue it with hedonistic intent. I was raised to hate that lifestyle but now that I rejected Christianity I didn't worry about it as much. Rich people bothered me; I don't know how they can live with themselves having all that money and doing everything they can to keep it. I am not jealous at all it is just what can you do with near unlimited money that you can't do with a decent amount? It just seems ludicrous and pointless at some point and it just becomes narcissistic to fill a house with possessions and have such luxuries while others are starving. The moderate wealthy aren't who I loathe it is the builders of the great skyscrapers

I pass in the city such tall buildings and in Africa people live in huts. The industrialists poison the air and pay politicians money so they can continue doing it. It is the people that take resources from other countries so they can continue to grow and collapse and then grow again. The people all around would have enough if we leveled the whole world out and chose to equalize the wealth spread it and what not. You get the idea, big hippy dream. The song Imagine in a nutshell. It doesn't seem it should be difficult. It's like Michael Bakunin says that people gain such wealth they lose their hearts and mind. Ramble, ramble, ramble that is all this is.

Well anyway to my friends, yes they were wonderful. There was a girl named Melissa. I met her in front of the school bookstore, she was at a table and trying to get people interested in Amnesty and I jabbered on and shit about how great human rights was and told her I have heard of Amnesty and was actually a member before I joined the school group. I learned about Amnesty through music allot of less mainstream artists liked Amnesty. U2, Joe Strummer, Radiohead, Rage Against the Machine were all into Amnesty International I believe. I may have mentioned it; I don't remember, doesn't matter. I remember being all depressed before about not knowing who I was but this gave me some hope I think. I talked to a friend over the phone allot about my sexuality and my confusion about it. I think I mentioned that it would be neat if I could be this girl's boyfriend but I didn't realize she was already with someone else at the time. I made a joke of some kind though there was a table adjacent concerning soldiers or the military and I said "Isn't it funny how they human rights table is on the "left" and the military one is on the "right"?" She laughed a little bit and that was a small victory on my part I said in my stupid head. She was great though so responsible for being so young I continued to think as I got to know her I thought to consciously on some ranking system "Oh no she is too good for me." I thought but this did not matter because she liked a wonderful boy named James.

Now James was in the group too, I think he was more involved in the school's U.N. club or that is what I initially thought but he was also very helpful in our Amnesty group as well. He was someone else I could talk to, I could talk to all these friends they just were such a great group of people, so intelligent, in fact on occasion I felt dumb around them because they talked at length about some things in detail. I could rant but the details wouldn't be as specific and I didn't like to rant in front of people. I saved that activity for when I was online. Anyway, James was real tall and he was handsome too. He had a nice short beard and clean shaven face but not entirely, it looked pretty good and his glasses were nice too. He was a great guy not a misogynic ass in other words. Misogyny was about the worst thing ever I could think of and if people didn't fit into that categorization I could tolerate them. I did more than tolerate him but loved him like a good friend should not in a lustful as I had decided I didn't think I was homosexual pretty sure I was a transgender lesbian in a man's body but then I guess I would be heterosexual in a sense if I loved another man.

There were others that came to the meetings but only one more that went to the first trip. Her name was Lenna and she was a great person too, very smart just like everyone else. She was a self-proclaimed socialist and an atheist. She was into science, and majored in the classics. She talked about her boyfriend allot but I never saw him except once and that was on her camera which she brought with her on the trips. Lenna talked about sex and the health benefits of it and made me think I was really missing out "it's fun and good for you" I thought. It seemed like she traveled allot because she mentioned plays that she would see in other states. Sweeney Todd was one mentioned and I talked about how I loved the movie with Johnny Depp and would probably like the play. We talked about all the bands we liked. We both liked hipster bands or stuff that was less mainstream I think most people do but for some reason don't admit it. On the first trip we talked at length about all the bands and stuff we liked. I think that is how we connected best. I still remember her saying there was something she didn't like about I but she didn't know what it was. I am not sure either but I thought it would have to do about just how I threw names like Chomsky around and didn't attach much evidence to the claim. I didn't talk about specific contents about things I don't know like she thought I thought I was smarter than I was or want to act a certain way that I am not. I really don't know the exact reason or perhaps not anywhere close to the mark but I thought she was a fine person anyway.

There were others who were at the group; they didn't come because of prior engagements. One of them didn't have their mother's permission, another was complications with a parole officer or something; I didn't know much about it but I guess he sold marijuana which shouldn't be a crime but I will not rant about that now. Melissa said someone else may come and her name was Katrina, she I don't think ever appeared at any of the meetings and didn't really know who she was but she ended up actually coming to the Chicago trip. We made plans and arrangements for the trip and all that and the time we would meet at school to go; I was actually real early and I didn't expect to be. I was reading a novel by the clock tower whilst waiting; it was Albert Camus's The Stranger. It was a great book about a man who murders another but doesn't have any motive to defend his action; he kills a stranger and was thrown into the whole situation without premeditation. I was reading allot of existentialist works at the time I will probably read more. Philosophy class got me interested in existentialism. It is more innovative yet also limiting depending on the school of existentialism. I enjoyed Jean-Paul Sartre; so did Lenna she noticed in addition to Camus I had Sartre's Transcendence of the Ego and she said she "had a little crush on the man". She read liked The Stranger too said she read it. I started reading books late or later than I would want to; if I could go back in time I would tell myself to read a lot of books. I tried balancing political, books about wanderers, and philosophy with fantasy, horror and political fiction. It was hard to do, there wasn't enough time. I wanted to get good at instruments and play them for people use lyrics based on knowledge from books and write books inspired by other books, protest using rhetoric and fact from political books but I wanted to be confident with all my talk and stuff and I always forget the details. It was an absurd mission; I didn't ask for it I was just a stranger armed with the knowledge all this knowledge at the wrong time in life and could become the artist or intellectual I wanted to be. I sighed and huffed through it not everyone is perfect I thought as I think Bukowski said "Everybody shits". That's another thing Lenna didn't like Bukowski, I suppose that is fair he was honestly an asshole but his life was rough and I found a kindred spirit in him, plus he just had a good sense of humor I thought.

Well everybody was there at the school and I saw Katrina for the first time. She seemed pretty cool. She smoked and I didn't mind that, my parents smoked all the time but she smoked with style or perhaps I liked to think that. In addition to being a pretty girl she had cool clothes and a great sense of style. She wore a knit cap and not just t shirts like most kids usually just wore t shirts and jeans including myself but I wanted to develop some sort of style I kinda had a grunge thing where I wore t shirt, jeans and flannel. It was better when my jeans were ripped. I liked to add necklaces too and I guess that was enough. My folks didn't smoke with "style" they just looked miserable; Katrina looked like she didn't care or like she was a stereotypical French person in a movie at a café. I don't know people say French movies have people just smoking at café's I don't know if that is true. I know the French invented Avant Garde art and film and though I didn't know much about it was at least interested in it. I listened to some music with elements of it. Frank Zappa, John Lennon, Yoko Ono, The Velvet Underground, and Sonic Youth all experimented with it I believe and I liked most of their music.

Katrina seemed to know allot about things like what people did in the city and stuff. She knew how people acted and has been around. She was the only one to have visited Chicago like actually visited not just a drive by. She wanted to meet her ex-boyfriend in Chicago or I don't know if he was even her ex. She wanted to see how things would go with him. I still don't know the entirety of the whole situation, I just know that a lot of things were on her mind about it and I didn't know anything. I never knew anything, I only knew what I wanted to and that was mostly concerning me. I was a hypocrite, I was so introverted and said I wanted to help people and this and that but didn't want to get to know anyone too well or explore the possibilities and expected it all to come to me on a platter. I expected women to come to me I didn't want to go to them and I thought I was fuck ugly because women don't want to be whores despite all the fools that say they are I have never had women whore by another man without the man taking the first move. Women are judged as prude if they don't play along with the misogynic game and are judged by old people and their peers afterwards of being a slut because she will be judged anyway. It's a double edged sword as Allison from the Breakfast Club says. Everyone knows it somehow no one is pissed off. It is probably, because they are all having so much fun accepting it. I hate all the fools, all the fucking bastards. Well I guess we are on our way now.

CHAPTER 3

From Ohio and through Indiana

So we were on the road again. Just like the first conference but now with an extra passenger and headed straight out of Ohio. Ohio was an alright state I guess but I liked just about every other state more than it or at least the ones I have visited which wasn't much but I assume it is at least better than any place like Alabama or Texas or Tennessee. I assumed all of those states were full of rednecks which still seemed to lurk here in Ohio up north. As you can tell I have a little thing against the redneck community. One bullied me in high school and I bullied him back everyone was real proud that I did it; I don't know why. There shouldn't be a reason a redneck is a bully up north. I thought they were the fucking minority here, I guess not in the country anywhere. I desperately needed a city to live in. It was apparently expensive and dangerous but I don't care at least there is more culture in the city that is what I want. People aren't ignorant assholes like in the country. I wanted to get away from fans of country music; I just couldn't stand the crap and if I wanted to be a musician I would have to go where people liked rock, alternative and punk.

We kept along the freeway. I always hated freeways so open nowhere to look but to your sides where you could see the trees. I would rather look at trees than the horrible stretch of pavement along the road. So much money went into roads I thought and often wondered how horrible it honestly would be without them. I came to the idea it wouldn't be so bad. It seemed like they always fixed roads that were fine and wouldn't help roads that needed repair probably because those roads were in poor neighborhoods but would it be so wrong if the other neighborhoods helped the poor ones out instead of funneling it into the repair of an already fine road? I know it is probably more difficult than that.

There were no trees though it was spring and they were supposed to be blooming but only the evergreens had their coating. It rained a little bit but nothing too serious. We stopped by a rest area and went to the restroom. On the last trip Lenna was really into collecting coins from those machines that you put money in to make money with a picture on it and not an old dead white guy. We joked about it and tried hiding the view of these machines and succeeded this time actually. We got Starbucks instead and we talked of hipsters go to Starbucks but pretend that it isn't Starbucks and we had a good laugh about that. We went back to the road and into the state of Indiana.

Indiana was pretty forgettable; it just was allot of open fields and farmland and stuff like that. We went to another rest area and there were several knick knacks that exploited their folky east Yankee redneck sensibilities. There was lots of stuff with deer on it and concerning the killing of animals, hunting in other words. I guess it wasn't as bad as what they do in the factory farms if it isn't being killed simply for sport. Killing for sport is plain vile and savage. Call hunting what it is killing. That's what I say but no one really cares about that especially in Indiana apparently.

Lenna and the others looked around for postcards and stuff. I don't know if they got any in Indiana; it may have been like a joke like "hey we went to Indiana and this is what we got." Indiana didn't seem very special and I think I made that pretty clear anyway so I suppose I will not dwell on it any longer. I just was anxious to get to Chicago I think and our rears were killing us for sitting in the car so long.

We passed the toll booths and got the tickets and paid the tolls and all that. It didn't really make sense to me why they needed tolls to cross over to some other part of the earth that looked mostly the same. It just seemed absurd I guess and I always thought thusly. It wasn't a big deal though really because it wasn't all that expensive.

We stopped at some gas stations we tried to get more ethical gas than BP but there didn't seem to be many Sunoco's around. I didn't really know the specifics about why Sunoco was better but everyone heard about the BP oil spill and their irresponsibility with that whole situation. Melissa was really big into doing things the most ethical way possible. She got vegan food and made sure it was all fair trade. I got fair trade when I could but there weren't many places around where I lived. We had to buy cheaply made things because that was all we could find. Melissa was amazing in that respect of being so devoted to that principle and I really respected that.

I remember bitching about my parents a little bit and talked about how they just would be over protective and not let me do a lot of things. This trip was a break from the status quo just like the last one. I can mostly blame myself because I never was into getting a driver's license. I was still kept away from a lot though and that damaged my curiosity in making me want to find different things.

We listened to some good music on the way. I brought the music but the others liked it so it was all good. I brought some Velvet Underground which Lenna really liked that I brought it. Katrina I remember wanted to hear "Candy Says" so we played the cd from the box set that had that song. I always liked the song and thought it was real great, it seemed to have a melancholy yet peaceful feel to it and I just really liked the sound it had. Despite liking lyrics to songs and all that I don't really know the words to that particular song by heart. We also listened to some Atoms for Peace and also some Beck which kinda made me feel like somewhat of a hipster liking all this not so main stream music. We also listened to some Against Me and Radiohead later and that was great and everyone seemed to enjoy it and I loved that they were enjoying it.

We were just about in Illinois and I remember hearing it mentioned how Chicago was drastically different from the rest of the state. Katrina mentioned how she wanted to see that boyfriend or rather ex-boyfriend of hers that she was considering getting back together with or something. I was bad with understanding what went on when people talked of relationships and things of that nature. I never had a romantic entanglement with anyone and I just sort of blocked details about other people's engagements from my mind so I wouldn't feel so bad about myself. I don't know if it was healthy to do my parents seemed to not mind it but occasionally my dad was very into the idea of me dating someone like I had to prove I was a man by applying my lusts for relationships and I always got the strange feeling that I should marry anyone who even gives me a chance. It wasn't realistic and that is why nothing ever happened because I was always afraid of maintaining a relationship and I never wanted to break a commitment if there was any chance of one happening and I just kinda over thought everything about it. I was afraid of what might happen. I thought if they said no which would mostly be inevitable because if I asked if I could go out with someone it would most likely be half assed and not committed because I was so positive things would never work for me. People would be like put you out there but I didn't see myself as special and wouldn't want someone to endure a relationship with me. Acting romantic seemed too demeaning to me as well it seemed so bleeding corny like it just happens in the movies and shit no one is that sentimental. I think that is why I cried during romance movies because it was so fucking stupid things never happened that wonderful way in real life and it sure wasn't at all going to happen to me. I was going to die alone; I was sure of it. I could not afford a sex change to feel comfortable with my body and with another woman. I would be on my own. I was surrounded by a climate of ignorance and I couldn't get a damn license to attempt escaping the ignorance and stupidity.

I would often think all dressed up and nowhere to go when I was out somewhere and those were the lyrics to the Against Me song True Trans Soul Rebel. I loved the song I just really connected to it and it made me sad. Could I be a True Trans Soul Rebel could I take the stares? It gave me hope and hopelessness and I was just hoping that one day I would wake up in a different skin. I didn't see much point to life without love or a partner to share experiences with deeper than ordinary friendship and family, a conjoining of the soul whatever that means. A union between two minds and without fear you could share anything with them and felt completely comfortable having sex. I always thought sex sounded a little bit gross and I hated my penis I didn't want to put it into a woman's vagina it just seems so terrible, I know women like it but I can't understand why.

We got to a hotel by Chicago perhaps it was in Chicago I don't remember but it was pretty nice and we unpacked everything and made plans about where we would go from here. We didn't want to go eat anywhere too American and that was decided. I don't know why I just didn't like it and ethnic food was always better and most of it was more ethical too. We decided to dine in an Italian restaurant.

Uhh... Chapter 4

Well we unpacked in the hotel and I think we had to sneak someone in because we didn't all come in at the same time. The room had to under my name because I was the oldest. It was weird because most of the time I felt so young like I didn't see much of the world, in other ways I thought I was really old, because I concerned myself with international issues and politics and stuff such as that. I was an activist, sorta, I mean I gave money away to organizations that were supposed to stop all the horrible things from happening. I liked going on trips like this it felt invigorating to see all these other people that seemed to be concerned about the same things. At the last conference we signed petitions for different causes so that it would nudge governments to stop doing things. I always felt so disconnected with all the things going on like I wanted to pretend to care about all these things but felt I couldn't unless I saw these problems happening in front of me. It's like my problem with god I can't believe it if you don't have a sense that anything is there. I don't need to see him but I need to feel the effect. After all I did say I was an empiricist. The only problem was I didn't experience anything on my own accord; it always seemed I had to rely on someone else and money was always a problem how could you live your life bumming around and trying to be some sort of revolutionary. I was also afraid of my ignorance and that is why I read all the time. I wanted to immerse myself in this knowledge and the god damn awful way things were but then I realized I was still living and doing nicely but that was because I was all idea and no action, if I tried mixing them I think I would be in trouble with some people. The NSA might have a file on me but I assume they mostly ignore it due to my lack of teeth and balls.

The worst thing of all to think about is what if the left was wrong and what if people are just naturally assholes and the only way to survive was to be a bigger asshole. Some "liberals" were big assholes but they were better at hiding. They pretended to fight wars in the interests of democracy and the people within the countries but all the countries our country supported were tyrannies and suppressors of the population. The past reveals we were great friends with our enemies who mostly continue the same practices of today but we say they are good now because they do things in our interests, our as in the United States, and by the United States they mean in the interests of the rich and everyone has heard this rant before, everyone knows or I assume most know. There are people that say being a tyrant is how the U.S. should be after all we live here we should support our home, others are like what the hell can you do there is too much power that these rich people have we can't do anything, there are the people that think they can make a difference through the system and influence the governments to be more caring for the population even though these things go against the interests of the people currently in charge, there are people that don't think about it and watch American religion, the tv set or the Sunday Christian go to church every Sunday act like an ass all the other days and perhaps not even the entirety of that day, the fundamental Christians that only care about riding the world of abortion and homosexuality all the other issues these people could care less about, the active democrats who go to Obama rallies and support him like a king, he acts like he is a liberal like them and everyone eats it up, the conservatives who listen to the radio man day by day and complain they haven't gotten much loving and take it out on homosexuals saying they are these great abandoners of morals when in their heart I know they wish they could fuck all the women they want maybe some men too but they have to stay rich be a gentlemen or act like one until debates on pro-choice and pro-life come up then they spread their chauvinism as they ignorantly tell all the women with unwanted children to stop spreading their legs, yeah there are all kinds of people I know them but I am not them I don't know their lives, how they grew up, I understand how people were conservative, their bloody father probably was and complaining about Clinton and all that and the bureaucracy of things and I admit it sounds like a drag and I get all of that but the reason all this stuff is so hard to get to is because there is all this other stuff going against the more direct human help people need, it's like everything is an exchange and it's all about making a buck. The guy offering people insurance and coverage so they are safe in case of injuries it is all disconnected and shallow. My dad talked about all those things but I still turned out a liberal. I started thinking in terms of war and what we have to protect here and I thought what is the point of the state and what is the point of the place I have my feet. I can go anywhere but I felt I couldn't because the society pouring it's problems on my tabula rasa but my innate mind told me there was something beyond it was just, it didn't seem right, nothing seemed right with the devotion to something, it was like football and baseball teams, there was no difference between that kind of devotion and nationalism than to the application of the state or the countries we lived. We were all people and animals and living things we were this planet. It seems utopian but I really could never grasp these concepts, I felt like an alien I didn't understand this way of life. This uncanny devotion to things, I wanted to find a place to be devoted I thought it was for human rights and all these liberal intellectuals and artists that I read about that I listened to music of revolution and would say to myself someday, some day it would happen and then what I would think and then all was black.

Well back to the hotel we all unpacked I had a uke and I played a bit. I played a David Bowie song, The Man Who Sold the World and I also played some of a Beatles tune All My Loving both great songs. Melissa and Lenna had ukuleles too, they didn't bring them but I let them play a bit. We decided on a restaurant after the uke session or whatever and we decided Italian like I had mentioned before, you saw the reasons you heard the rant. I am not American I can't associate with that. The land of opportunity for those rich enough to buy it, a capitalist state in other words, the mass production capital, the modern industrial revolution out of control, crash bang it's ok it's our right to kill, they won't kill if there is no one to kill the bad guy, who is the bad guy, the guy without the cash, they are bad. Oh really oh really poor people don't decide on war they know nothing about other countries they can't go there. It's just like me but I ignored the spoon feeding that the media sent these people want to destroy us and kill us and if we don't kill them first they can't do it to us. A kid on an ant hill stepping on ants, the ants being lesser than the kid, the kid is powerful, the kid is tough and that means he is righteous but the ant has not much life to live insects typically live a few years or so the kid appears as a god to the ant but the ant keeps working and trudging over and toiling for some kind of objective. It dies and the world still turns but it turns because they are supporting each other the ants are a colony and they do what they need to. I don't know exactly how they help this world but they must do something. I didn't think about any of these things at the time I was doing things and being happy with people that were easy to be happy with, such wonderful people if only everyone could be so delightful. We were then on our way to eat. Gorge on the dining of one of the first "great empires" of the world. I didn't think about it that way I just knew it was the land of endless greed, the U.S.A.

We drove around and looked at things nothing fantastic just some things around the rural town kind of areas of Illinois. We saw a Popeyes and IHOP and the others said that we were in such a poor area or something I didn't recognize it that way but I don't know I didn't get around much. Melissa I remember talked about how people called here Marissa. Even amongst all the friends in the car I remember someone calling her by that name on accident, we had a laugh over that. We listened to more Radiohead, the OK Computer album to be specific and that was so great to listen to it was the last album they did without electronica influence. It was probably one of the wildest albums they had. It had some great subtle songs too and I loved those they were depressing and melancholy and I liked that music. Lenna's favorite songs were No Surprises and Fitter Happier. Everyone thought it was odd to like Fitter Happier particularly it had some music and a voice that sounded like Stephen Hawking in the background speaking of the philosophy of the basic boring human being. I talked about the song Electioneering and how it reminded me of my professor's U.S. National government class and how politicians do their campaigns, the chorus "You go forwards and I go backwards and somewhere we will meet." I noticed it with campaign of Romney against Obama. It was real noticeable with Romney, he kept changing his positions he didn't do it right, it was so obvious to me but not to most people in my family. No Surprises was great and almost sounded happy with the peaceful sounding ring of the Ed O Brien's guitar riff but Thom Yorke's lyrics and singing changed that. The song reminded me of my life and what I didn't want to continue living just this mundane picture of subhuman existence and life, the rejection of an existentialist way of living. It was a beautiful song though and it made me picture also a world, a simple world where people didn't have to worry about other human beings a rejection of modernism or industrial modernism rather and a world where people were socially acceptable and decent and no one was untrusting of another human we would have "such a pretty house" and "such a pretty garden" and "no alarms and no surprises". There would be no untrusted handshakes and less carbon monoxide and we wouldn't have to worry about it all coming down. Well anyway we were pretty much at the restaurant and when I got in I was a bit unsure of the place because I noticed a soda dispenser and it looked very fast food we went to be seated in another room and it was nice though and I was relieved.

At the restaurant we were served bread, you know like at the Olive garden only these were not sticks they were slices of bread. I asked for some Merlot to go with my Italian pasta. A couple of my friends decided to have something not so quite so authentic Italian. One I remembering ordered an eggplant burger which sounded pretty good anyway, it didn't sound to American for some reason Americanism really bothered me and I think you've got that already. I don't even care it is just some kind of principal really I know eating American food doesn't really support America any more than our taxes do probably much less in fact. My parents always complained about taxes. They complained about it going to welfare and schools and hospitals you know all the good places it's supposed to go to but I think allot more goes to foreign countries, for guns, bombs and our roads domestically but the roads it fixed didn't need fixed and the towns with shitty roads were too conservative with their money to care about sure annoyances but the richer areas that had the money would waste it to fix roads that didn't need fixing. I always thought it would be spectacular if the different towns or cities helped the poorer towns out with their shit roads and all the roads looked nice and not just the good ones that were re done every other month. Apparently this was some sort of dream. I don't know, this wasn't something I thought about then just a reflection of America and what I saw happening.

Lenna wanted all this butter to go with her bread and this was funny I don't know why exactly it was just a peculiar thing I guess. Melissa asked if her meal could be completely vegan and without cheese and instead for extra olive oil I believe to use on her pasta. I had cheese on my pasta I was vegetarian though but I felt like dairy didn't harm the animals I told that kind of lie to myself to keep eating cheese. I loved cheese and many dairy products. It's wrong I know but giving up meat was good enough for me then. We made jokes about James and Katrina and how they were assisting in animal murder by eating meat with their pasta I believe they got pasta I kinda forget though. We talked about the past too and about school and this show called Community. I never saw it myself but it was about college and we had to see it apparently because we went. We talked about the books we read in high school and how much they sucked in contrast to what we read now. The Outsiders and That Was Then This is Now to me were ok I guess at the time but in all honesty they weren't so great not nearly as good as my dystopian fiction like 1984 and Player Piano. I also loved fantasy like Lord of the Rings and James really liked that and all of Tolkien's literature, the books were too long for most school students though. My favorite school book was The Picture of Dorian Grey and am surprised I forgot to bring that one up because that book didn't suck at all. It just really got inside my head and I finished the thing way before the due date, it was great so poetic in it's phrasings I thought and most books didn't seem to go that way. Most people at the school didn't like it they didn't like the homo erotic implications within which honestly I didn't notice too much maybe it is because I didn't care. I talked also about how I liked Stephen King and mentioned the list of his books I read and James said the scariest book of his was Pet Semetary. I agreed either that or the Shining. They all had their moments for me. Pet Semetary was scary because you could tell how personal the story was for Mr. King I read the introduction to the book and it mentioned how most of the situations actually were very much the same. He just added the bit about bringing the dead to life but the Pet Cemetery was real and the stories of the road that took the animals out. The scariest part of the book for me was the dream sequence with the ghost fellow and the main character I forget his name following him to the Pet Cemetery I believe and he is falling into the graves and wakes up with all the mud and stuff on him. We mentioned how the movie wasn't so great in comparison he said his dad loved it and I liked it too; it just wasn't as good. That was how most movies were in contrast to the books. I loved the Shining and Clockwork Orange those were the only movies I think that were equal or perhaps even better than the literature. I loved being around friends that liked literature most of my other friends in the hick town Jefferson while not hicks weren't too into books, they liked video games, so did I but I wasn't a gamer so I couldn't discuss them like they did. Lenna didn't use all the butter and shoved it in her purse I think we had a laugh about that. We needed boxes. The wine was good and then we left. Good diner. Good conversations. It was good time in general. That was only the beginning.

CHAPTER 5

Through the Streets of Dead White Men

We continued down through the streets of Chicago; they were all named after dead white guys, we spoke of this in a humorous light at the time. One guy was Polk the U.S. president no one knew but he had a street. What about the people tortured by the police of Chicago most of them being African American didn't have a street named after them. We learned of this later on at the Amnesty Conference. We protested against the police of the city but that is for another time, as of now we just drove about.

Katrina wanted to see this guy she knew in Chicago; he had an apartment in the poorer area of the city. The others were a little bit nervous about the poorer regions of the city. I didn't dwell much on it. It may have been due to naivety or I just didn't care what happened I was in the city and there weren't rednecks. There probably was some angry poor city folk looking for an easy buck though and who can blame those people. It's the land of opportunity for the thieves, the cheats and those born into it. I also thought dumbly "hey we are progressives and not snobby rich folk we don't look down on people" that was true but I don't like I said how can you blame the desperate for what they do. You can to a point I guess but I rather point my finger to the thieves in the skyscrapers and the glass ceilinged tombs of which the wealthy have made their home. All concentrated at the top the pyramid of hierarchy was becoming bloated at the top, producing more and more to line their pockets. The material possessions forming a height the tip could not support the large expanse of the bottom had to do something for something to give and stretch out into all the world. Hammer sickle tattoo gleams in the pale light of a parking lot. Katrina showed the tattoo we have a communist in the car what a cool thing I kinda suspected anyway. So selfless I would later discover. Explains allot. People don't get communism they think of Mr. Stalin in America when the name of the ideology surfaces not of Karl Marx or even John Lennon. At its heart it is not meant for a global totalitarian state it is the freest system; essentially it is pretty much Anarchism with a different name. The fields are level everyone has what they need not a gluttonous amount but what they need. Selflessness something political idealists like Ayn Rand hated. Capitalism hated it and said the interests of your self were greatest good, the interests of yourself conflict with that of others. An anti-social climate wanted. Emile Durkheim had statistics about suicide numbers mostly due to poor social engagements. Protestantism being a branch of religion with the most suicides and a religion that made capitalism popular, capitalism bringing about industry and the industrial revolution and alienating the worker from the product from their mind from other minds, just slaving away not with a hammer or sickle but the push of the button, the pull of a lever, the thoughtless actions of a machine in movement, the crushing of human morale, the emerging of revolutionaries like the fine Karl Marx but minds need compensation because the opportunities aren't open for thinkers just doers and it isn't very much let's not forget Fredrick Engels, he gave Marx the money he wanted but let's forget about that. Can't get anywhere without the almighty dollar, need it to help the rest, need it to exploit the rest a paradox, it is a catch 22 and there is nothing we can do. Workers unite rise up against the mighty dollar the specter of communism in the air can you hear it not over the yells of the right on the radio on television set in your mind in your head, do you see a future or is it dead. Blah blah blah. It's all words and means nothing to me but also everything catches 22 all over again. Catch 22 Catch 22. It's a book I've never read but an expression I've always heard.

Well anyway enough of my ranting's. On with the plot or my journey and the rest of our lives my life and everybody unless they are dead and it's a different story always subjective and always a subject what happens to the dead? Where do they go if anywhere? Is our life a dream and do we wake somewhere else when our life escapes our bodies. Do we ascend into heaven or descend into hell. To the ground forever in the ground matter created only to never be destroyed. This world an endless wheel spiraling around the ideas emerging and creating an evolution of the human being are we destined to be free one day but never be satisfied always inventing ourselves like what the French fellow Sartre talked about his school of existentialism and he was a Marxist fellow too. The direction of our vehicle is going off into the ghetto city, the land of the scraps where the rich lay their crumbs. Most of them are fine unless if they face an injury or an unfortunate accident, accidents that arise because everybody is untrusting of what everyone else wants. It is not the money but what they get. Basic pleasures advertised and drilled through the new religion sitting home watching television. They don't need the wealth just the safety. They aren't jealous but want to live well. Well, being content so they can learn have more free time to get ahead up into a point of human potential which would be extended with the human capacity to think. The capacity to think do people want to think? Is it in their interest? Increasingly in the capitalist society it is not so. You want sex and violence that is what makes the money not metaphysics and political theory. Is there a meaning to anything I suppose only to create meaning? Ah Existentialists, the hopeless romantic of the philosophical world. Thinking something can be true but never accepting something that is all too good. I was a romantic and only accepted love if I knew it was staring me in the face for sure. I gave up on true love though as soon as I no longer believed in God, your parents would always say there was an Eve out there for you but if no God was out to provide there you would have to be your guide and despair and wallow endlessly for someone to tolerate you enough to have sex with you. I wondered what it was like for homosexuals to hear there was an Eve for them, if they liked men would they just have to live life without company. It's all in your head the Christians would scream to the homosexual but the call of the lord god almighty would miss the target. God is gay he doesn't care about anyone else he just loves himself but maybe he is two sexes in one but honestly probably is sexless but we human give him one to identify with him. The men made it a man and the women had to or else they would be rejected. As I read about god through different perspectives I became increasingly fonder of Satan. Paradise Lost was a good spring board. Off to the ghetto. Off to hell.

It wasn't as bad as all that. It reminded me of Gotham City probably because Batman Begins was filmed in Chicago. Two of my comrades were worried about crime, one was perhaps neutral and I and Katrina were fine. She held secure with experience and me with my blind sense of curiosity. We stepped outside in the cold wind of the city near the address of Katrina's friend or whatever he was to her. It meant allot to her she said that we were meeting him. They hugged as we entered. He was a cool guy from what I noticed. He told us to be at home and stuff but we refused due to sitting down so long during the car ride. His apartment was cluttered a bit but nice all the same. There was writing on the walls or a wall rather like graffiti or something like it. The guy introduced himself but unfortunately I forget his name he was dj though I remember that and knew another cool guy that did art like pop art similar to like Andy Warhol. I liked to think I liked allot of art and stuff like that. I liked to look at it and think about the possibilities of it and what it could mean and what the artist was thinking or what he wanted to get across and stuff like that. I didn't look at weird avant garde stuff and say "that isn't art" I tried to appreciate it whether I did or not could be subjective, I mean I liked it but perhaps I didn't understand it "properly" or wasn't able to put what I felt about it into complex phrasings or articulate words. I just liked it. I only went to an art museum once and it was free. I remember looking at Salvador Dali's stuff and liking it quite a bit it just looked sorta trippy and dreamlike. I remembered a Picasso work of a man playing a guitar and

I liked that an awful lot but not just because the man played guitar like me, there was something neat captured in the image I think and I just like to think I connected to it. We planned on seeing an art museum in Chicago, I hoped we all could go and see the spectacular art that would probably lie within. Art meaningless yet so meaningful and different kinds of art too some not even would hang in a museum some in writings. Art is any creative way of expressing the soul whatever that is. People said I was gifted at drawing but I didn't think I was and I didn't pursue it far but I did like drawing musicians and strange creatures that looked like they were from the Pink Floyd movie, the Wall. I wasn't bad wasn't great I just drew stuff; I thought I was better writer but I suppose it is mostly subjective. Artists never think they are good and if they do they start to suck at art or at least that is what I think. Banana man stand made of wood right in the guy's apartment he said it was some of the work of the artist that he mentioned. He had stickers too. Melissa asked for some; we put it in the amnesty office we had for our group at the college. Bananesty, a pun, one of many that would endure through our travels. I liked the puns I guess, they were so silly and ridiculous amnesty this and amnesty that amnesty everywhere and what a good thing. Making amnesty into pop art putting out in society in the minds of others by attaching it to everyday objects or just anything seen in pop culture, the idea wasn't in mind probably but it planted a seed in mine I suppose. It's kinda funny a commercialized sort of label for something against the interests most of mainstream culture, I guess it's ironic if it makes at all sense to anyone reading this. The Banana man immediately made me think of the Velvet Underground and the Andy Warhol banana cover and all that. I was sure that was on most our minds because we all were somewhat familiar with the group and all have probably heard of Andy Warhol. He could get allot this art from this guy and liked it allot. I liked it too. He had a friend over not the artist just another guy that seemed pretty cool and we shared names, shook hands explained our business here in Chicago which was the Amnesty International conference. He went outside for a bit to have a smoke with Katrina and we talked to his friend and now ours because he seemed like a good person not an ass at all. Most people if you bothered to talk to them were great people.

He came back in after the cigarette and showed us his other friend his dog. It was a nice dog, a pit-bull. He talked about how all the hippy dippy people would be worried about it but it was really a nice dog the breed had a bad rap. Everything was great as you learned about it. Ignorance courts fear and fear courts anger and stupidity and you've heard it if you've seen Star Wars and heard Yoda talk and all that Jedi Buddhist religion type stuff. He said that Chicago had some great places to eat and talked about how it was that way because of the liberals and hippy dippy people who liked more ethical eating. In other words, there was less meat heavy dining. I noticed a magnet on his fridge that said not to find yourself but to create you. It isn't relative to anything in the moment but I didn't forget it. He talked of how he loved the dog and said how dogs really love their masters and mentioned how cats expect it and think they own their owners. I never exactly thought of cats so shallow but I don't know. I also mentioned how my dog acted allot like a cat because it was raised in a house mostly with cats. We agreed on the socially structured environment and how that played a role in things other than innate natures of things. I don't completely believe in Locke's tabula rasa idea that all minds are blank slates but am sympathetic to the idea and agree for the most part of it. We had such a good time there and we chatted a bit and then left in a fairly short amount of time altogether. Katrina thanked us for visiting the place and I didn't mind I can't speak for anyone else but I don't think anyone else did either. It was a nice visit and I enjoyed every minute, every second of it.

We left and traveled the roads of the dead white men. The roads were absent of colored men's names and god forbid a woman's name be there. I didn't think of it at the time just a reflection. All the buildings we passed more reflections of the bloated corporate system of the United States were they so united? Not at all but that is what the country was called anyway. An image of unity on the surface order is what you are supposed to see and for the most part there was a kind of some sort but I could not forget the disorder on the behalf of the curtain of order that was supposed to remain. The cold war's where blood ran out hot from bodies shot at by guns of the savage governments and terrorist regimes but I never forget terrorists can exist as governments and I always said the America was one of the biggest terror states of all no one believed me but the choir I preached to. No one sees what happens just the roads of the white men that died fighting for the ideas of this "great states" and "land of opportunity". Martin Luther King usually had roads places I remember seeing them but he was a godly man therefore also listened to by the establishment. Religion and the state; they are linked and not one person can convince me otherwise. I've read

Michael Bakunin but I don't think I needed to, to make the distinction. Karl Marx said it was the opium of the people a sense of security, something to make them feel they could be safe after their heart gave out and the generations after should be ok upon establishing that humans are meaningless creatures and altogether awful because of Satan or because of God or was it just themselves there had to be some cause I guess in all this. If existence precedes essence something must exist before what comes after it. If god is all powerful one must assume he intentionally made people able to be ass holes and why would he do this. All suffering begins with life but who can have happiness without suffering. The good things seem all the better when we have shit happen to us. It still doesn't make god right for creating assholes but I don't believe in god. So I won't gain the benefits from the lord our god or whatever. God didn't create the state in his image that state created god to support it.

We went back to the hotel for sleeping. I slept with Katrina not in a sexual way of course we were just friends and it was obviously understood but for some way I had to remind it by saying I don't expect anything when she said I won't try anything. I always had this stupid thing about self-pity and about how everyone didn't want to have any sex with me. I pretended not to care while trying to look a bit like I cared. I didn't understand what I wanted to gain from it. James slept on the floor because he was such a nice gentleman and all that and the Melissa and Lenna slept in the same bed just like me and Katrina and then there were dark dreams.

CHAPTER 6

Chicago, the Marriot and Amnesty

We woke up from our slumber. I was dreamless can't speak for everyone. I had a good sleep though, good meaning that I actually slept and didn't toss and turn and all of that. Again I didn't have any dreams which I guess means instead it was an ok sleep instead of a good one. I liked dreams because they served as inspiration for my stories and I tried to make sense of them like and apply what I saw to my life. It's like a different kind of application of empiricism the unconscious state of empiricism or perhaps another consciousness I thought. Apparently people had dreams every night but I only had them on occasion I was almost sure I had nights without dreaming only pitched black. I remember some dreams that I didn't remember but these nights were different. I did not mind nightmares because that made good stories and I knew they weren't real, they couldn't happen or were they happening? It's just a dream just a dream I tell myself without conscious thought but what if it is something more. Nonsense I cannot feel sensations in those states but what if those realities don't allow such states of feeling. Oh what whatever never mind.

I was awake before anyone else I was just reading my existentialist novels. I had with me the before mentioned Albert Camus work, The Stranger and short stories by Jean Paul Sartre. I also had a novel by Franz Kafka, I never read the whole thing honestly, and it seemed decent though. It was about a man who turned into this bug and he was alienated to the world due to this. I was not alone when I read the book, I could relate in some way to it and I think most can in some way. I especially felt isolated I was an alien to society, a transgender female, a slave of the slaves. I am oppressed by my insecurities that are projected onto me with the public's insecurities. Nobody knew I was transgender except the people I told but I still felt the pain of rejection. All dressed up nowhere to go stuck inside a skin that doesn't feel quite right and no one understands. They sympathize, the people who aren't assholes but I don't want to be a charity case. I don't want to be a leper messiah. I just want to live like a woman and love women without feeling weird about it. Get over yourself my parents say, when they eventually find out. They don't fucking know I am not shy; I love conversation and don't differentiate because of someone's sex. Asperger's my mom says no son you're not crazy you are just autistic fuck you, fuck all of you. You can't tell me how to feel. Nobody can nobody will. Fuck everything; fuck nothing so I won't look so pitiful it's all about fucking in the end isn't it. How liberating it must feel I can't imagine. Who could complain when they are fucked unless it is rape? Religion probably keeps it from people to make them sheep and like they don't matter. In high school it was a mob mentality, you were nothing if you didn't fuck and even if you didn't lying and pretending like you did counted for something even when everyone knew you were full of it. I never lied I was ignored which I suppose is what I wanted back then. I opened up later but then it didn't matter. Did it really ever well I guess I must decide on what matters after all I am an existentialist and I must make meaning out of what seems like a meaningless life.

We all packed our things up and started on the roads of the dead. The roads of the dead white folk but you already heard all that. We wanted a parking spot by the Marriot hotel that Amnesty international was using for the whole conference. Our rooms were cheap enough but parking was pretty expensive. Driving around the city was great; I liked the big buildings and also hated them at the same time. I thought of the people suffering to erect them but how wonderful they looked. People along the streets, some seemingly hopeless and asking for change as in money not hokey Obama bullshit. Activism and protest not hard to find in Chicago. In Chicago, citizens with pure hearts, the wealthy have soaked the blackness out so the blood is seen. They are ready to fight. I saw two or three men wielding signs reading "Hope" it made me believe there was some. The masked avenger known as Guy Fawkes or V spoke the silent message upon the sign. A crazy old man sitting with a sign saying something about the president and whistle blowing. I didn't know what to think of that man, is he a crazy tea party ranter is what I asked myself. Regardless it was democracy people speaking their mind about the established "order". People never did it in Ohio it was refreshing in Chicago; I loved that about the city. Ah liberalism, democracy, hope, freedom, peace, amnesty, all that great stuff in the air.

I didn't really think about many of the Chicagoans on the trip many of the people there may not have even been from Chicago. In fact many times we asked these people directions either they didn't know their own city at all or they just weren't from around there. The only people that really stuck out were the protesters which I assume were from Chicago, the friend from earlier did mention how many liberals lived in Chicago.

I was beginning to notice something about Katrina and how she was so pleasant around people. I am not saying it is unusual to be pleasant but she was very kind to complete strangers always complementing their clothing and just typical things such as that. She did it everywhere and it was so genuine I liked being nice but I was actively nice if that makes sense and if I was being actively nice it was through some disconnected thing such as charity or donations. We were both altruists but she was really altruistic. She would have made Rand go mad. I have my opinions of Ayn Rand some bad and some good. I agree with her opinion on redefining selfishness and how if used for rational interests self-interest is a moral good but that is subjective to linguistic analysis or depends on what one determines a selfish action like if you do something for another out of the irking of your soul or heart or whatever technically it is in your self-interest but not necessarily selfish. I think if you act generally great towards people that would influence the rest of society to act the same way so I don't think it is really so irrational to put others first and in the long run I don't necessarily think it is against your own interest. Anyway I was just really impressed by her attitude about it especially because she was responsible for driving and smoked and stuff. It really made me want to change how I acted around people. I just wasn't sure how. I suppose just do it.

It took us a bit to find a parking place in fact we ended up having to park on a roof of a parking garage. It cost allot but it was alright the hotel was nice and cheap because of Amnesty. It was very windy up on the roof; in fact that particular day in general seemed quite windy and I suppose this is why they call Chicago the windy city I thought. We took an elevator down with all our bags and had to use separate elevators because all 5 of us with our bags couldn't fit in one. Level 5 was the level we were on; I believe they also labeled in Eurasia level or something which reminded me of 1984. It made it easy to remember what floor we were on; I suppose it would be hard to forget being on the roof and all. We checked into our rooms and it just so happened we were on level 5 at the Marriot too. Lenna or somebody said that "that should make it easy to remember" or something like that and no one forgot imagine that not too hard I guess.

There were paintings in the hotel hallways; I mean there were some painting in the other hotel but these ones were actually pretty nice. It was quite hacky artwork is what I am saying I guess, you got the feeling that they may have wanted to be artists or did rather than they were making it to hang or look like scenery or something. I hated scenery art so fucking pointless; I am not much of an aesthetic when it comes to art. You know art for art's sake; I mean I like art that tells stories or is trying to get something across and looking nice can be a bonus but just art where you have the idea they were just looking into the distance and copying nature or something just so they could recreate the scenery just seems dull to me. I mean there has to be some significance. Well anyway we got to our room and there was neat art in there too. There was a fridge and everything cost something nothing was complimentary. They had cans of Pringles and if you had them they were like 6 fucking dollars or some shit. You could ask for a bowl of cereal for room service and it cost like 6 dollars too. It was ridiculous. You would have to be some rich bastard to not give a damn about tasting anything in the hotel. We didn't have anything we brought our own snacks.

We got ready for the first Amnesty meeting which was a protest demonstration; my first one ever in fact. We met at the tables a floor above the first floor to get our schedules and things. They gave us calendars and dvds too. We got our name badges and I was identified as a Partner of Conscience. I didn't feel particularly special but the man that gave me the badge briefly thanked me for it. I felt ashamed actually not proud; I didn't do much I just gave money but I couldn't do anything no car, no freedom to roam. I guess it's my fault. Kids usually get their licenses when they are fucking 16 or 17 and I was fucking 22. I envied people who could drive not because of the vehicle or anything I never understood people and their strange autosexual bond with their vehicles. In fact for so long that turned me off to pursuing my license. It was where I lived damn hick town with all the rednecks obsessed with their pickups and shit. The shittier the better. That same perspective they apply to others. I realize not all redneck white trash acts that way; they can't all be racist, misogynic, ignorant, stupid, assholes. In fact actually that always pissed me off that people would get angry when I ranted on about such things but nobody hung a fucking neo Nazi from a tree no rednecks were targeted on such a basis perhaps they were attacked in self-defense but you never heard many people talk about hating them. I hear them talk about women and they disrespect them so much and they talk about how stupid "queers" are and they hate "pussies" they only like tough greasy sweaty not particularly in shape but not particularly out of shape men. Where is the prejudice towards the prejudice people I thought? I heard people bad mouth African Americans, Jews, and Asians but never a fucking redneck. Couldn't wrap my head around it never will.

So yeah we went to the streets and passed the old homeless man complaining about Obama. I don't like Obama but something about the man made me think he may have been full of shit and capitalist but perhaps he wasn't maybe he was libertarian socialist or democratic socialist or something I don't know and will probably never know. We stood out in front of city hall and we were later than most people but the jest of the whole thing was that the Chicago police were cruel to several people, mainly on the basis of skin color a few based on transsexuality. There was a mother there asking for her child back he was in prison and it seemed like he wasn't a bad kid his mother seemed fine, only he wouldn't be a kid, he was locked in prison for much too long and he was tortured by the police, he couldn't get any innocence back from that. He wasn't the only one there were many others one of the people was unknown that they tortured and some of their victims I believe ended up dying. It seemed pretty clear the police were wrong regardless; they had policies where they could just grab someone off the street without needing a warrant or incriminating evidence and just do what they wanted. It was a sickening thing to think about so I didn't. They held up signs for the victims and all of them were tortured and stuff. We were asking them to give the people they freed security after the unjust treatment a way to get back on their feet so they don't go right back in. They wanted to have the people get psychiatric help. It wasn't much to ask; it would cost the state some money but then again the state seemed pretty bloated with law enforcement. States never seemed to want to spend money on the less fortunate only the fortunate I guess or on nothing in general. I don't know much about anything it is just how things seem; like helping people was some burden but we needed to go over to other countries to save other people but even that claim was a crock of shit, it only put people in more danger when the military was involved other places. The crowd chanted some phrases after the speakers were done speaking about everything and for some reason I couldn't say a word. Yes, all this stuff was terrible but I was somehow so aware of how pointless shouting seemed in such a big city with all the noise everywhere but where else could you do it, you'd be put away if you did anything in a town or in some rural place. I felt uncomfortable for some reason like Winston in 1984 during the two minute hate I don't know if an O' Brien spotted me and saw that I wasn't part of the collective of which somewhere I desperately wanted to be. I stomped on the ground and even pretended to shout but I felt just really phony like I was so aware of trying so I just stopped altogether.

Afterwards I walked around a little bit as they talked some more. I saw a man with a petition against Gerrymandering. I knew I could get on board with his cause only I had to be from Chicago to be concerned with it I guess. He asked about the protest and I informed him on the whole ordeal and mentioned the other work we did, and that we thought to secure human rights in all faucets of life. It was international meaning we looked at cases everywhere every issue from corporate accountability to women's rights to LBGT rights to being against torture and the whole drone ordeal that was going on and international terror and yadayadayada. I am glad he was interested and perhaps he will be involved in some way with the strengthening of human rights but I guess it seemed that he was already doing just that. He was another one of the fighters for democracy and all that; I felt like an ass. I was being lugged around by others to pretend supporting human rights which I did but I need to experience it; I wanted to feel connected and not like only support through finance corporations did that for their politicians and they had a hell of allot more money.

We went back to the hotel after our ranting. I remember passing a man speaking to no one in particular just doing spoken word or something with a recording probably utilizing the things he saw in the city as inspiration. I saw another person being interviewed for the restaurant Chipotle; they were asked about why they frequented the restaurant they probably talked about why they generally liked burritos and whatnot. They were asked the frequency of their order and if they always got the same thing out of habit. It seemed so pointless to me really. The speaking word man or whatever eally. The cy of their order and if they always got the same thing out of habit they probably talkhe was much more interesting I saw these people at two separate times of day perhaps they were even seen on different days. I contrasted these two people one was probably doing it through artistic thought and the other person was speaking for a corporation and what they liked about it. I don't really understand what I really felt of these individuals they just seemed interesting to me and I am making note of it now; it isn't particularly interesting but it's something.

Well anyway, we got back to the big hotel some point in time. I remember James said that he felt uncomfortable in big hotels or maybe even just hotels in general and the immensity of them like it was an unnecessary luxury and I must say that I agree the hotel was immense. He was humble like a fighter for human rights out to be always sleeping on the floor for the behalf of others so to speak. He slept on the floor in the hotel rooms too but I think I mentioned that. We got together into a big room to hear people speak and they spoke about the cruelty of the Chicago police yet again and the growing gun problem that the youth of America were facing. There were some people at the meeting that feared gun control and some who wanted to get rid of the evil things. I am not sure who I agreed with more to be honest. I didn't like guns myself and didn't like the idea of killing even in self-defense. I believed that making it difficult for people to get guns wouldn't really help the problem though, people who shot people on a regular basis aren't going to get guns legally but I guess the people that seem normal that get guns may actually be nuts somewhere down in their head. The basic background checks seemed like a basic idea. It doesn't solve it though you need to get at the root I thought and ask why do people go out and shot people and I believe they do it because they feel trapped in the prison of mundane life and are looking for thrills and some out of desperation for them it's the only way for them to survive. The way to solve crime is increase the happiness of everyone making them not have to worry about the next day. A good start would be making universal health care for all so an unfortunate accident wouldn't put someone into poverty. People shouldn't have to pay so much into life but in a way they should strive for so much more. The only way for them to break free of desperation is find humanity. The people are alienated from their work and live in an industrial age of automated satisfaction for the slaves to consume. It is not enough the desires of gluttony or lust or greed. I think humans really desire knowledge and communication. I am not fooled by the fools they too I believe want to live and discover things but they are too desperate in the current situations to attempt learning for what can it get them? I echo the rants of ancient philosophers in this theory and wonder if it can still be valid in this day and age. I think most philosophers have the world basically figured out the best it can be to the human understanding; it is just their interpretations that are different and I prefer other interpretations over others but really all these things seem mostly to be linguistic differences and all amount to the same fucking hill of beans. They all come to the terms that the universe can almost never be completely known and they just settle for their nice little interpretation to apply to most situations. I like the existentialists because they put things in our hands and let us interpret our destiny they say yeah life is pretty much meaningless so it is up to everyone to figure it out. The meeting concluded and no new answers were found except the ones in my head that were probably somewhere in every other person's head as well. It is all so fucking easy and I can't understand the difficulty in the powerful to commit to the weak because I could never understand the attachment the rich could have to their power, all that education, all those riches and luxuries if they are still not content why don't they let everyone experience the same wealth, yeah they would be poor like the rest but the class hatred would no longer be existent no barriers against the others, no intimidation just all trying to explore the world and rebuild through scientific discovery. I only hope the tower of Babel story is false; I hope god is truthfully dead for if he isn't what is are humans but rebellious animals? I have much faith that god is dead. Who is guiding us; I feel none, I don't feel a power dictating lives except the one we have created on humankind. I sometimes believe perhaps we need this thing to resist against this halting of potential leaves so much time to live out our existence or perhaps it will be our ceasing of existence, perhaps we built our towers too high and they will topple and no one had a safety net to provide for such a catastrophe? Who will know will anyone, do we want to, oh what whatever never mind.

CHAPTER 7

Chicago, the Marriot and Amnesty Part 2

The hotel despite its great size had a limited amount of things that were enjoyable to do. We could talk and that was in all honesty my favorite thing to do. It is very feminine I suppose or at least that is what they told me, the collective whole of society but as Soren Kierkegaard said, "The crowd is untruth". It is not necessarily that they are untrue for that reason that they are the crowd but as an existentialist I believe that we must form our own lives and define ourselves rather than others making those decisions for ourselves. In the words of Nietzsche "God is dead" so therefore there is no universal moral guide to how we are supposed to act. The state and institutions and the whole have society has taken the mantle of the deceased and have imposed rules on the people but if there are a few dissenters then who can possibly be correct, the conclusion must be no one. The only moral obligation that reasonably makes sense is one of neutrality but also of extremes the denial of everything the great devotion to these ideas and increasing other peoples pursuit in creating themselves and to liberate. I guess that is why I was there in Chicago with Amnesty to spread awareness that all have the same rights to act and think as humans. We are responsible for these states if we wish them to exist for our security for the time being and if there is something the state does incorrectly we have ourselves to blame in the long run for we must regulate the people we put into power so they can't carry out what we see as injustices. It is only common sense to me. It is common sense to all but the "underman" as Nietzsche says to stay afraid and refuse to do anything fall on the state or god to solve these problems. I don't support his rule of "will to power" it makes me only think of barbaric attitudes of ancient times of survival of the fittest as Darwin and Spencer put it. The stronger survive and the weaker follow. The true way to liberate is to level the playing field and give equal access to all so they can collaborate without fears of superiority and class and all that they can just focus on becoming more civilized and a more just society. But this is just ranting and a dream of the current lives we live under capitalism.

Melissa had to go to some leader meeting for she was the leader of our school group, there was debate if I was to go but she forgot to mention my position of vice president so I didn't go. We grew tired of the hotel so we went to check out where the art museum was because that was something we really wanted to do. It ended up being pretty expensive and then I guess we didn't want to do it that much but we did check the gift shop out. I remember seeing books and knick knacks but my favorite things to view were recreations of some of the art pieces. There was the Picasso man with the guitar and Van Gough's Starry Night that everyone could just get. I really enjoyed Salvador Dali's stuff but unfortunately I don't think I saw any. Katrina got a postcard one with a painting of Dorian Grey that was very cool. I mentioned how I absolutely loved the novel the painting was based off of. Katrina noticed I was wearing a Bad Religion t shirt mentioned how she really liked the group and we talked about it briefly; she continued to say that I should have brought some along for the car ride. It wasn't dwelled on something I just remembered; I think I unconsciously didn't bring it for I knew that a couple Christians were present in the vehicle; most of us were atheists however and I am thinking now why didn't I and thought all about majority rule and how come I considered the opinions of the Christian ahead of my own, why was I unconsciously afraid to offend a Christian with somewhat anti-Christian messages and to boot they weren't even so much anti-Christian as it was about liberating minds. It was a punk band and the main goal was to spread ideas of revolution and individuality and shaping a better world. We left the gift shop; I left without anything, nothing I really needed.

After that we walked around and someone asked if anyone wanted to do anything else and I mentioned the book store. We all liked that idea and went to a Barnes and Nobles; it was in connection with a big college. It was a very large store and I would almost say the location would be like Heaven if I weren't so opposed to the conception of such a place. I looked around and was lost in the sea of knowledge and pseudo knowledge assuming there are probably books within that try to pass as having scholastic value. I looked at the philosophy section and looked for more Sartre to read I think but for some reason I don't remember seeing any Sartre in that section. I saw some Paul Churchland and Noam Chomsky though but I didn't get either. I didn't know much about Paul besides his eliminative materialism theory which I liked and I already had a bit of Chomsky and this stuff was just about language and didn't interest me as much as the political works. I went back upstairs in search of Sartre and Chomsky. I did end up finding some Sartre and got a whole collection of Chomsky's best essays in the Essential Chomsky; I felt so lucky and glad to have gotten these things. For some reason, the very fact of them being in possession of me filled me with ecstasy. I had a peculiar habit of collecting things, my mom joked that if I worked at a book store I would be completely broke due to my temptation towards literature. It was my heroin and every time I finished a book I would look for a new one to read. I wouldn't even finish reading them all before I got new ones my room became cluttered, yeah my mom was probably right about that. Eh, I guess I could have the self-control who knows guess it would be up to me anyway. The Sartre book I got was Nausea and Lenna seemed to like that she was a fan of Sartre too. I was new to Sartre but I liked his views.

Melissa was back at the hotel and so were we at this point. She talked about how Amnesty leaders were a bit stand offish and actually didn't want members to talk as much as they wanted to or something like that. It got me depressed; I felt abandoned by this group that I was putting my time into. It's about spreading awareness and Amnesty is helping us do that as long as we are doing that it's good and in addition these conferences are a good opportunity to grow as activists I suppose. I was trying to look at the good amidst the bad news that I had just received; I felt betrayed and it made me feel so bleeding dependent as well I've been so dependent all my life. It was in every aspect too that this trait followed. In relationships I hope someone would just rape me or something I wanted a woman to just force me down beat me make me her dog because I could never feel right fucking her. I felt uncomfortable with my penis; it doesn't seem like it should be there. I don't want to stick in a man's ass any more than I want to put it in a woman's vagina and vice versa. I never was a take charge person because I felt that defiled character to the nth degree. I was so conservative and I wanted to be liberal to liberate myself but I was relying on the words of intellectuals, the teachings of schools, the support of friends to help me and encourage me to do things and then I thought what is there to do, we are all dead and we will be and there will be nothing. The most I can do in life is think about things and I guess that is gratifying enough and to live the experience of life was a great thing honestly despite how full of shit it was and how full of it most people were. The people who lived reality were decently happy and decently miserable at the same time. That is the way to live within the golden mean I thought. Do not live in excess or decline of anything shoot for the middle which is an extreme in itself, I am not talking neutrality I am talking to make common sense I suppose.

I forget if that night we had another group meeting and I can't really remember what it was all about if it happens due to the prior information. I do remember reading more Kafka and about the bug that the man would become and he was in quite a crisis everyone was dying to get into his room but he was so disoriented and uncomfortable. He feared how other people would perceive this bug and he was behind that door I never read beyond that door; I hope to finish that story someday but I had to return it to the college library some other day. It contrasted my life as well this Kafka bug thing I didn't want anyone to get past that damn door because of fear of what might happen. I suppose it is like America's foreign policy "anticipatory self-defense" which I must say is a stupid thing indeed but why was I emulating it in my own world. If this style of strategy continued it would destroy myself much like the foreign policy would hurt the world because according to America we are the world. This is so fucking obvious I don't wish to dwell on it but people are so blind that is because they don't read but reading has brought me to wear glasses. Am I indulging in my reading too much am I going past that golden mean? Most certainly so but there is so much to learn I thought how could I possibly discover it all. So much damn information, I wish I could live forever and I don't want this world to end like all the Christians are literally dying for.

Christians are so bland; no imagination, their god is too small there is a vast universe beyond the moon and the sun. Heaven can't be the end. I don't want it to be but somehow they are content thinking in such a way. I will never understand the fascination they have with wanting to be sheep and god as the Shepard, it is such an obvious thing the government uses to control is through religion. It popularizes the idea of we are lowly people we can't achieve paradise by ourselves because we are awful evil people by nature tell someone something long enough it's true and what does that make me and you and everyone you know. Christianity is under attack they scream such a bleeding farce it is alive and stronger than ever and all the people turn to it. It is their government, vote for the puppet on the supposed left and the puppet on the right. America has an abundance of Christian leaders how is that so are they just better are they blessed by the god fucking almighty no the wealthy just buy into that kind of attention I know it; it has to be true and all the people swallow it up as these words fall on deaf ears their vision is all to good as it adjusts to the computer screens and the films and television. Such an advanced age with all these things we don't need our minds god will save us these computers will be our fucking life. We will be laid too but not through a passionate love it is just to get our fill it is mandatory. Everyone needs to get fucked that was the crisis in the schools, never bought it because I was Christian at the time and I don't think I would buy into it otherwise. Life feeds of relationships but not anymore we gotta get all we want but not what we need. It is a capitalist world now and we are doomed to die because of the crazies who do not like our way of life to drain the earth because we all should pursue our interests to the nth degree, we are the government but we need to suck our own dicks and if we are women we have no luck unless we suck the dick of another. Blow job that is the only job in capitalism, sucking other people's dicks. We can't rely on ourselves but we have to get what we can and cheat if we can't win but cheating is a sin so you just stay where you are with the carrot hanging in front pull up your boot straps and believe. Believe damn you Believe damn you. You are a lost sinner and a bastard son. A threat to the live and wellbeing of others because you want the fields leveled and anarchy to rise. You fucking satan bastard, stone the non-believer but even the demons in hell believe in our power we can't anymore, we can't anymore.

CHAPTER 8

The Greatest Night of My Life

After a long hard day Amnesty International decided that the students should have an opportunity to experience the night life of Chicago and they extended that invitation with the welcoming of its members to the House of Blues to hear some music from some bands. I didn't know either of the bands, they ended up being pretty good. Our group was mostly absent from the experience but it was a blast for the people that went. I was one of those people. The reason Melissa couldn't go or rather didn't want to is because she had duties, her duties being a test that she really had to study for, it was perhaps good that she stayed despite missing out on a good time, we jived her about her declining but it was all in playful fun, her boyfriend, James, didn't go due to the fact that Melissa didn't and Lenna wanted to stay and talk to her boyfriend who wasn't really with us at all. Chop chop slice bam time to get back to the point. It was me and the night and Katrina and the people in the night and the band and the drinks and the fun that is the focus. Target, pinpoint, greatest night of my life thus far perhaps not maybe so but mostly, if it wasn't I can't remember a better time at this moment through all my life.

We went outside to wait for the people leaving they left without us or we stayed without them, it was up to us to find the House of Joy. It wasn't blue there at all but anyway... well yeah I was asked where they were off to but I didn't see their path so clear I guessed the path that I think I saw them go down but they could not be seen pretty sure it was the right way. We came across a drunk man with no clue but he tried his damnest to give us directions to the House of Blues, a kind soul really but misguided or perhaps guided so great without much consciousness, he was awake but stumbling around, silly and unsure but who is and he didn't claim clarity but who should no one. The man kept pursuing us asking some things, he was getting a bit too friendly I suppose asking our names but I think we asked his first or Katrina did anyway, she had this kinda thing about getting to know people ever so slightly in the hustle and bustle rush of this start stop go when they say lifestyle and you gotta have a job get what you can and the bank closes and too bad for you holy shit it just hit the fan scat bam whoosh and there you are alone no friends so I guess you got to make them as you go along make yourself up as you go yeah yeah yeah that is it, never ending spiral down the drain or out into eternity and we were nowhere lost in the man's knowledge his trek our trek my hand was held for security for comfort perhaps I felt well but it was a façade but deep down I hoped not but I never hoped too much and what is there to hope at all but hope itself? People watched I think but didn't buy it were about to sign the check but not cash in whatever I don't know and like I said who does we were on our way in the lighted city in the living night, night more living than the day time people were more themselves unless they had a nightshift. You could see those people too walking quickly in the nice clothes with a case in their hand they tried their damnest not to see people they just saw the torch but it was all the way in New York on the Statue of Liberty if a torch were in Chicago it might blow out being that it is called the windy city but sometimes it isn't so windy really. They looked like zombies, I suppose they were the walking dead but they could also sit in a desk at a cubicle answer calls and say words not just groans they saved that for morning and their times alone not under the eyes of the bossman perhaps they would curse him I don't know never been in a cubicle job never will not who I am or rather not who I want to be.

Lost losing our minds but not really we would get there but did we really know I didn't know the city really but Katrina knew more about places and people. I just read books about people and sometimes it was only abstractly about people and just governments and the terrorism against people by previously mentioned government and yadayadayada well anyway other people were on the street to ask questions. "Are you local" meaning around here we would ask people were confused by that for some reason some people didn't seem to have the time, some were just assholes or perhaps not I don't know someone eventually pointed us someway but it was wrong yet again in fact the drunk guy led us in a very new direction very much the opposite of the House of Blues, the second person led us the wrong way as well as we later found out from some kids who knew the city, they looked like decent kids about our age perhaps a year or two younger but we are all children of the world of the universe I guess all made up of water and molecules just like everything when we figured that out we could soon depart because we found the way or nirvana or something but we might have to convince more than just ourselves. So we could come back and preach these things again once enlightened I don't know all that Buddhist mumbo jumbo but in small detail I like the Buddhist way but I am not convinced by everything therein; it's a hell of allot more comforting than Christianity one chance only hell or heaven you choose but how do you know if you fully chose who knows, the preacher man I don't think so fuck him fuck them all but they don't want anyone fucked they want you in their hole. Buddhists want you to live but only sometimes and Christians want you to walk around and try not to live. We had to get a cab or rather it was the best option around being that we were so far from our destination. We thanked the man allot when we entered the cab or rather Katrina did I just listened to the thanking and agreed about it in my heart or whatever and perhaps would say something if nothing was said already but repeating spoken words feels a bit silly if it's something so trivial as a thank you but maybe that is important to some people. This guy was a cool cat though he had some Miles Davis on in his car. Listening to city in the city watching cars go by and all the lights it is just ah it's living without living it's watching life go before you eyes and accepting it. Bitches Brew was the name of the album by the way. I thought it was Miles Davis before he told us who it was after Katrina asked him, she was talkative to people she didn't know like I said before and I admired that I guess probably because I was not at all that way and it was something that didn't get me angry. He was excited I think when we mentioned the House of Blues; he probably liked blues in addition to jazz.

The guy was real laid back like I said before he was hip. He perhaps smoked marijuana; it wouldn't surprise me I guess. He dropped us off we paid him a bit extra because he was so cool or the fact that we really needed the ride or perhaps just to be nice. It could be all three for all I knew but I knew better than that.

We entered the bar slash venue slash restaurant to discover that we hadn't missed anything at all yet. The band neither of them had performed there were two bands if I forgot to mention. The first I hardly noticed but I'm getting ahead of myself we are not there yet but now as I write it has past but how is it still there because of memory and I think therefore I am and consciousness can prove that things happened. We are sure of this, pretty sure anyway sure enough to say I am pretty sure anyway and I was having a good time or had a good time whatever you prefer to hear it's your reading pleasure that's right I know your reading this if you picked it up and read this far into my experiences, they could be all false you don't know. I do know however and now we went to grab a seat the both of us me and my imaginary date never had one in my life but don't feel bad it doesn't matter to me it's just how I wanted to live. We sat by these guys from Rochester, New York or that is where they said they were from we mentioned they sat behind us at the Amnesty meeting I don't think we did, they didn't remember we were just trying to start conversation they didn't know perhaps they did they seemed a bit confused but we had a brief chat about where we all came from their friends came and then we left to find some other people to sit by. We found some folks from Colorado and they were more talkative; I wasn't so much, I hated being quiet I needed a drink and I got one a Vodka with Sprite it felt good going down my throat almost felt itchy I guess very delicious loved Vodka it was my drink didn't care much for beer plus I liked to say it was tacky or too white trash to drink it. I liked the idea of Vodka for some reason I liked to pretend I was a depressed Russian revolutionary fighting against the Soviet system, an anarchist like Mikhail Bakunin. It was stupid but something I did anyway. I also enjoyed wine but I never had any at the house of Blues and the band began to play or a girl with a guitar rather and some weird twat that was introducing them tried to make himself sound interesting and to make a long story short he was not. He drug everything out about the artist and thought his voice was art but it wasn't it was annoying perhaps that was part of it to make them want to hear the band instead of the rabbling. Finally he finished and a girl played guitar and sang and someone else played violin it was nice but no one paid much attention. I didn't really both I was listening to how our Colorado friends came here and they didn't stay in the hotel they stayed somewhere else. Some people from the table came and some left perhaps to talk somewhere more quiet about something. I was left alone with mostly alone with a girl from Colorado, one of our new found friends, I don't know if it was a set up or what. Oh yeah I forgot to mention me and Katrina talked about my problems with relationships before we got there it was small talk that was brought to life by an action I did at one of the Amnesty panels I made exceptional support when they mention transgender people and homosexuals at it and how it was for those who supported them and who were apart of that community and I was a bit shaken up for some reason trying to speak about it when brought up on those Chicago streets maybe because I didn't like talking loud all the wind and the cars and people all that played a factor in my discomfort at that point in time but I tried saying I basically wasn't quite sure but pretty sure however I was transgender but not quite sure I mentioned I liked women though but thought I was a lesbian and didn't feel comfortable being with women in a sexual way because of my penis and broad shoulders and all that. I was pretty unsure though and seemed a bit dazed in my response and I wasn't even drinking anything before we came. In any event I felt that my current condition being alone at the table with this girl was some set up for a date and I was thinking this was fucked up because she was so hot and I just was nothing and I wasn't so smart or not as smart as I liked to think I might be in certain occasions but I was stupid now because the music and the people all the people in the house talking I had to talk so loud and I hated my voice. I kinda mentioned what I did at college I wanted to focus on my novel writing because it was more impressive to me it was out of the ordinary and I didn't know what I wanted to major in I was just kinda there to learn anything I was drawn to politics and stuff of that nature though the liberal arts and all that stuff. I for some reason could not explain my first novel for the life of me or at least in great detail I must have sounded like a fucking retard but at least I was writing something and got it done and had a vague idea of how to get it out there I was chatting with these internet people on a website that claimed one could publish their stuff. I told an overview that was very poorly explained I said something like "It is like a very philosophical novel and it's like realistic but it isn't like it's like science fiction but not in a traditional sense most of it is based in the real world and I mentioned how the main character was all aware of everything while others were in the dark" and that explanation is almost generous to what I said. God, it was pretty embarrassing ordeal the other came back and the other band was beginning the man spoke again and we waited for him to yammer up but he kept describing every fucking instrument on stage. The band started it was all reggae and I liked that. I had a thing for it I asked Katrina if she liked reggae to be talkative and stuff she liked it decently she said. She liked ska and punk and that was cool because I liked ska and punk as well but I liked almost everything too. Pretty much everything but country for me, she said she had a brief country phase with some guy who liked indie but for some stupid reason was drawn into country shit and she just kinda started liking it which I can understand I guess if your around something long enough it can grow on you I guess. She didn't really like it anymore though. Is this really important to remember? I remember it so I am writing it down.

Everyone was dancing and having allot of fun we were just sitting decently enjoying the music and chatting but chatting was hard because of the volume of everything. We got up and I got some more Vodka, I think my third glass but this time with cranberry juice, good stuff. We stood by the bar tender just talking to each other a bit more on our sexualities she said she was real open with hers and I almost interpreted it as a way to turn me on and it did, there was activity in my pants and no one was invited I was real aware of myself and the fact that I was getting pretty drunk and the Whiskey that Katrina offered me didn't help lessen it.

She asked if I had whiskey before I said yeah I didn't tell her I wasn't crazy for it but that was perhaps because before I took it straight without any ice and warm and it was just too strong with ice it tasted great and I was having a great time nodding my head to while she was talking. She talked about having a bit of a lesbian phase but it didn't end up working when sex was a brought up. I was just getting turned on more and she wasn't drunk enough to make a move and I suppose I wasn't or perhaps wasn't comfortable was it ethical obligation for me I didn't want to take control to take advantage of a drunk person but I felt helpless to do anything I didn't feel so drunk because I was all to aware of my utter drunkenness, slurring my speech but for some reason my mind wasn't cloudy in fact it felt clear, clear of worry and I was watching myself and I was waiting for someone to make a move and I knew I wouldn't perhaps she would feel so bad for me she would get me to fuck her but I didn't want to not now perhaps not ever everything seemed so bad in the mind I wanted there to be more connection more than a drunken mishap but nothing happened like I wasn't drunk enough. Waiting for restroom invitation and we hit the dance floor and I that swept my worries away we both started dancing to the reggae beat and it was perfect to dance to drunk I really got into it and shook back and forth and when that excellent crash of the drums came I poked my arms forward like machine guns back and forth back and forth I remember watching Joe Strummer moving around to the Clashes reggae beat jives and I tried to imitate that in my mind and on occasion I tried to move my feet almost like in capoeira fashion to the beat of the music while also moving my arms and body the guitars, bass and drums. I utilized my whole body I felt real proud of myself for some reason. I was having allot of fun dancing with everybody in the crowd. So much fucking fun I wish I could have felt like this all the time and wish everyone could be this way all day but the band has got to stop and it did but they played one more song. I could have sworn I heard the bass line to Police and Thieves and thought that would be just great because I could sing drunk and merry too but I didn't know these words but I liked the music. This song had like a special kind of movements that everyone did to it and it was neat moving as a collected organism but also we made ourselves up as we went along it was allot of fun. They got finish and packed everything up. I talked to Katrina after and mentioned how great I felt after all that dancing and stuff and she said bye to her new found friends they were my friends too but I didn't know their names but they seemed like a nice group. We wanted assistance on our way back to the hotel but the assistance was just older people who were just as wasted as we were and it was great and hilarious. I just kept snickering under my breath with this weird little hissing noise and laughed at these professors at colleges talk about other professors in their college and how anti-amnesty they were so racist and stuff and anti- Muslim. Katrina said something about it being an Abrahamic religion just like Judism and Christianity and it was stupid they couldn't get along somehow it was a dream for people to think that way and it was so hard to understand to me or these professors I guess you would have to be a fundamentalist Christian, Muslim or Jew to understand. Jews didn't even support Israel for the most part Israel ran under Zionism and a nationalistic devotion to the state of Israel and they drove out all the Palestinians to the Gaza strip and slaughter them and their children the building their economy, their hospitals in ruin, the schools too what else could they learn but their Islamic faith and naturally a hatred for the Zionist people not the Jews it is deceptive they are not anti-sematic they are just defending themselves but no one knows no one fucking knows. It doesn't really help that we gave terrorist groups so many weapons back in the days of the 80s when we fought communists instead of radical religious people which was mostly a lie too because we just seemed to kill allot of innocent civilians too and this only boosted the support for the unruly terrorist guys who were apparently the bad people. We only went after the terrorists because they were after something we wanted not our freedom but resources. I wish I brought all this Chomsky talk out to the professors or the people in the House of Blues it may have been more impressive than what I was just for the most part pretty quiet not shy though it was mostly the noise that kept me quiet. The professors were interested in what we majored in I said something stupid that wasn't even a major I think I said literature because I was writing stuff but I don't know I should have said I didn't know. Katrina was going for political geography which was a more interesting thing to say.

We came safely back to the hotel and said good bye to our new friends and went to find our room on the fifth floor of the Marriott. We were loopy laughing all the way to our room I was hissing under my breath chuckling and occasionally letting out a high pitched giggle it felt so fucking good to laugh so much and be like this; it was the one of the best nights of my life. I didn't want to fuck anyone

I didn't care about any of that I was just having a great time and Katrina did too I felt a bit bad for having her pay for my drinks and the taxi and everything I think I offered something but she declined because she was just nice like that. We woke everyone up as we giggled on into the room. It was so funny we were thinking don't wake anyone but that thought was funny and we started laughing everything was funny it was like being high I can't understand sad drunks or who could be mad while drunk or sad; it was a great feeling. They laughed at our condition and Lenna was glad she didn't go she hated reggae music. She said it was too happy and it was happy we were both very happy partially because of drinking and also the dancing and the music and the togetherness. Melissa said she wished she had come I don't think she got anything done that night actually. We had the time of our lives though. I was so happy, happier than I have been most my life; this was living.

CHAPTER 9

Chicago, the Marriot and Amnesty Part 3

I woke up the next day with pain in my head not as much however that people I assume usually complain about during hangovers. I had a hangover it was a minor one or perhaps people complained too much about them; I wasn't sure which it was I can't read people's minds. I was up again before everyone and was ready to get started with the day ahead. There was an Amnesty panel going on downstairs they even provided breakfast but that breakfast was in limited supply I had some fruit, I suppose I can't blame them I was a bit late. They were talking about this new focus they would be dwelling on which was discrimination of people who take jobs as sex workers. I don't think I quite understood everything about the situation, I could tell Lenna was interested she seemed interested in sex related things. I remember how she said something about sex being healthy for people to do, was I going to die young I thought due to the engrained belief I never would have any and save me save I would scream inside my head under the influence and with another one under it so much they would care for a drunken fool but I couldn't lose myself no matter how hard I tried reminiscing about that night, where was Katrina she wasn't at the panel getting something from Dunkin Donuts not too far from hotel, an everything bagel I believe. Marissa and Lenna were there I remember and they also talked about this new way to start actions and do activist work and whatnot. This site called ARK I forget what it stood for but it looked promising I still have of yet to check it out.

Went back to room I don't think we did too much but I remember waiting, I remember Katrina said something about the societies placement of women's roles in society and how they are disadvantaged. She gave some examples from her life, they were pretty personal so I guess I don't feel at liberty to discuss them. I don't think that she would mind but I just don't feel like talking about it, all you need to know is that it was mildly trying to listen to for just a moment it tugged at my head and my heart it made me connected to the situation and understand what I was there for, for all the human rights and stuff. Most males don't really understand what women go through I always liked to think I understood more, I think I did in fact understand women better than I did men because I didn't really understand allot of male chauvinist ways and how one would become to act in such a way I can't see it even whilst under that kind of influence I don't understand hound dog male macho pigs, the bastards and they say I'm the freak, oh he's a queer he isn't completely obsessed with breasts or tail he doesn't watch porn or anything well maybe some gay porn the other peers may have whispered or thought in their minimal capacity of their so called minds. Fuck them Fuck men I fucking hate them... Well most of them. James was nice.

There was extra time we had to check out the tables for certain actions and things there were petitions everyone could sign and send to governments but it seemed inevitable almost it's like you had to answer to the government and beg them please stop all these crimes against humanity and why the fuck was it even happening in the first place. They don't want to stop, they know what they are doing and we know what they do. We think the same thing things at the same time but we just can't seem to do anything about it but then there are so many of us and they are concentrated in the towers and skyscrapers away from all the people to struggle under their reigns sometimes we steal fire from above but as long as they stand some people will still be fucked and they don't care. I don't know if they honestly think they are doing what is right for everyone or it's all for themselves. If they think it's good for people they must be the stupidest fucking bastards in the world these powerful people like a meat headed macho man all brawn no fucking brain, everyone hates him and loves him at the same time. I sign the petitions anyway hoping that they will make some difference free someone from illegal detention, stop the drone strikes in Pakistan, and these wars or the things that bring them, the desperation of people, the death penalty, the state thinking it has right to kill, the state isn't even human and that makes it fine just like the drones we can't see it but someone pulls the trigger, or the plug. The hope that gays, lesbians and transgendered people become more accepted by the whole of society, why did it take so long for it to enter a global conscience of human minds, it was not even discussed intensely until fairly recent within this world's history, it's fucking embarrassing and women's wages aren't equal to that of men's and nobody's fucking yelling nobody cares not even women themselves they just turn the other check like Jesus fucking Christ as the crown of thorns is placed upon their heads as they hang on the whims of their source of income if you can hook a rich man you can make it yourself why can't you fucking do it yourself most women don't think completely like this anymore but it is still a cultural thing in the U.S. It makes no fucking sense to me any sense at all. The stupid fucking kid from the concert yelling about the fucking band was there yammering on about different panels. He sounded like a circus man calling for a big attraction, he was just corny to me I liked Amnesty but this guy I don't know he got on my nerves a bit. I was getting ready for a panel dedicated for artists who use their talents for activism and James was interested in it for he was an artist. I was an artist too I guess but not a very good one. I liked to consider writing a form of art and I played some instruments but I wasn't much of an artist at all with them. I couldn't improvise or us much of what I learned in different ways I mostly just covered songs, sometimes I would play around and try to make something. I wrote lyrics but I couldn't put them with the tune I was playing the writings were a bunch of ramblings sometimes and sometimes the lyrics turned out stupid and I felt dumb trying to sing them. I still was interested in this "artivism".

At the panel they had a rapper who wrote songs and had a group that encouraged other people in Philadelphia I believe to do the same. He was pretty good, rapping wasn't particularly my genre but he rapped about some deep shit and it had substance. I liked Rage Against the Machine, they kinda mixed rap and metal and I liked that too. This guy had a song about the Treyvon Martin case which was a complete atrocity; the George Zimmerman, shit head wanna be cop killed a kid, the only evidence is that the kid looked suspicious he had no reason to pursue him he went to act like a big man when told not to by his authorities and got the shit beat out of him, what a loser I thought he can't even defend himself he is a fucking grown man and this Treyvon was a kid, he was on football team but I don't know I don't think he needed to use a gun to defend himself and I think he should be better trained to not kill the guy and he didn't get a sentence nothing and some black woman gets in trouble for threatening someone with a gun but she never killed anyone. He had a song about Troy Davis, a man who was wrongfully detained on no evidence or at least substantial evidence if any; he was put on death row I believe for nothing. He mentioned Israel's racist atrocities with the Palestinian state which I am glad he mentioned no one seemed to mention terror we supported not even with Amnesty, there was mention about the drones and Guantanamo that is terror come to think of it. All of it was fucking inexcusable and only a few people here hated America I think. Some people even came from other countries which I thought was just great. Some of them I was sure didn't appreciate America's atrocities.

Two more artists presented their artwork; one was a political cartoonist that focused mostly on immigration problems within the U.S. There was another artist that was an amazing singer, spoken word poet and performer. She was amazing she started singing that she was human as she crawled down the aisle between everyone's chairs and broke into an amazing spoken word piece that was improvised I believe and it was a really powerful performance, I wanted to see her after everything to ask questions, I think James did too but I don't think either of us did have that chance. We walked out and around and back to our room on the fifth floor.

Throughout most of the day I felt very distant from Katrina particularly for some reason it was especially weird because we talked and had a great time yesterday. I didn't understand my feelings perhaps it was all the drinking but I didn't feel that was where it was at I wanted to know if my perceived come ons were truly that like if she was truly flirting or inciting an invitation or if we both were just drunk reading into the looks and letting out phrases that probably not meant to come from our lips at the time. All the talk about how sex was healthy for the human body Lenna talked about and Katrina was aware of the information Ii had some abstract stupid notion of believing there may have been charity at work and I may have had an even greater night or perhaps it would just make it worse probably the later for it would open up so many complications. I didn't really talk to her much until later that night but I will talk about that later. We had other meetings to go to and lunch and stuff we were very busy today anyway. Some leaders in human rights talked and stuff. There was even a surprise speaker, Edward Snowden. He was a former CIA agent and contractor for the NSA; he released classified documents to the public and got in trouble for it. He was disturbed about America's Big Brother policies and wanted a stop to it like all of us at Amnesty probably did as well. He called for everyone to be active in activism; it was encouraging to me and I assume most of the people who attended. He seemed more committed than some of the Amnesty leaders there because like I said the leaders tried limiting members' opinion from what I heard from Melissa.

We had lunch and it was very nice I forget if we had it before or after listening to Snowden. They messed up my order and gave me chicken I didn't eat meat. They replaced my dish with something vegetarian and it was very good. It felt pretty classy having lunch in a hotel and one like this. I picked up a newspaper that was on one of the petition tables and it was about the dictatorships in Central America and America's involvement in them. They didn't seem to talk about these things so much which bothered me. It's not that Amnesty were "too American" it was just more they ignored much of the foreign policies we committed. They did mention drones however and the bombing of children and a grandma in Pakistan though which was something. Well anyway I enjoyed my meal and then listened to some people; they talked and I listened not remembering much of what was spoken. Those words fell on my death ears I did hear them but I dreaded that I did not take in all the words and act out all that was expected. Despite all the unity I felt so alone and there was no community between me and the rest of them. I was unable to create relations with anyone I couldn't, I had no confidence in maintaining the relationships with these friends I had no car and didn't have a license everything was so inconvenient for an activist grounded I felt so guilty and what could I do I was surrounded by an environment that encouraged me to remain grounded. The world was too dangerous they said but I didn't care about that I want to face these storms but I need certain things and for some reason I just could not reach those things. The most I could do is rant every day on Facebook and say America is so bad and give reasons for it and shared links with empty quotes that fell toward dead eye receptacles that ignored the message of tolerance, and revolution, the links were seldom read and when they were it was like preaching to a choir because some of my friends already agreed with me. I enjoyed when a dissenting conservative would argue because I could show off my smarts and they could never win but I could never win; their mind was always to clouded by patriotism and conservative bantered rhetoric. I gave my money but not my time and it's not enough and nothing changes it all remains the same but it seems at this moment all I could do was hope and that is just another empty word.

We split up with each other I went with James and the girls got massages well the other girls because I like to consider myself one and perhaps it's just another empty word. We walked out to the streets we planned on checking out another book store; that book store happened to be closed however. I started talking a bit about last night and my confusion; he may have not wanted to hear about it but it was just starting conversation and all that stuff that keeps people sane. I said how I wasn't sure if she liked me or was drunk and I talked about how I was thinking her about her through most of the day but I didn't want to talk about it. It was a weird alienation that was created through myself and my upbringing; I despised it. I was open now however, couldn't keep my mouth shut I just kept yammering on about oh she might have liked me but I don't know if I was too drunk or she was drunk or a combination of the two and it was basically in that kind of strain. I knew that I didn't truly like her I was just wanting to like her and I guess I could say I liked her, she was wonderful but I didn't love her I didn't love anyone and I didn't believe in love. I thought I did when I want young singing along to Beatles songs and all that but no, it was not true and if all you needed was love then my ship is sunk because love is another one of them empty words that I was ranting about. Love is tolerating someone and not feeling stupid around them and sex is something that you can consider for a moment but for some reason later when your hitched it doesn't feel good anymore and nobody even brings it up and it is completely out of the question because we can't have kids that is just a bigger burden, then use fucking birth control I thought and they said no it is just not proper. They don't even fucking kiss or snuggle, they almost fucking hate each other at times and I think it isn't love at all. If that is love; I don't fucking want it.

I started talking about how I was transgender I think and how perhaps that wasn't where it was at and perhaps it was ferocious Christian upbringing; we passed a church by the way it looked scary. It was big but then all the buildings were but I thought a church shouldn't be big they should be small and humble but no religion is a business in America and the state needs them any way to preserve the status quo. I saw a sticker of a dirty looking old man it reminded me of the song Mean Mister Mustard by the Beatles. I don't know why but that was the image conjured up when I saw it. I took a picture of it and titled it Mean Old Man. I saw another sticker on the side of a light a little bit away and thought it was weird like it could be like a secret society like the Free Masons or Skull and Bones or the Illuminati but that is nonsense I soon thought but the thought is still here today. As I walked by that nasty church I mentioned how Buddhism sounded allot better to me than Christianity I knew James was a Christian but I didn't figure it would offend him and it didn't. I talked of this time I actually visited a Buddhist temple. I said it was really neat and the meditation made me feel allot better and I learned more in that one moment than several years of church. I started going on about how I went because of a class that my mom took on religion, I mentioned that after the excursion to the temple I did a bit of reading on Buddhism well only a basic book on the subject and a book by Bruce Lee where he talks philosophy and Buddhism and Taoism was a big part of it but he deviated from it a bit. I continued on about how I loved my philosophy course I was currently taking in college. He asked about what school of philosophy I considered myself and I said I was mostly an empiricist and believed somewhat in innate ideas and not the tabula rasa theory of John Locke which I actually used to believe in but I changed my mind mostly based on Noam Chomsky's views on language which made allot of sense. He talked about how Katrina has been through problems and whatnot and I understood that and it made me more unsure about the whole thing and thought was I just a pawn to fill a void but I believed she was better than that and knew that wasn't where it was at. Experience was the main thing I got out of the talk I had to experience more but I felt so limited to do it I thought. I needed to get out of this place not Chicago and not right now but I knew I needed to make changes. We talked about nothing in excess and I mentioned that that was a very Buddhist idea and that may have brought us to that conversation. Before I knew it we were back at our hotel.

When we got back we went back to our rooms I got emotional during the walk and tried whipping the tears away and they were gone before I got to the 5th floor. I told James he was great and talked about how great everyone was it was stupid and cliché and I don't know why I said it I was just calling out for some kind of sympathy. I was pathetic. I settled down for a moment and talked to James about music and stuff. He was real into metal and I said that I liked some of that but mostly was into punk, alternative and counter culture 60s music. I liked jazz too and Katrina came in talking about this jazz club called the Green Mill. She heard about it from our new found friends at the House of Blues and I thought man how amazing an opportunity perhaps but I knew nothing would come of it but the thought did arise. I was so excited but no one else could come Marissa had her test and James wanted to stay with Melissa and Lenna wanted to talked to her boyfriend in a different state so I guess I was just going to be with Katrina again. This time it would be jazz and not blues. What happened soon was rather ironic however.

CHAPTER 10

The Green Mill

I was so excited to hear the great news; I absolutely loved jazz, well apparently from what I heard it was a jazz/blues club but I hoped for jazz, that is just what I felt like at the moment I still loved blues however. Had still a bit of a head ache or I wanted some more alcohol or something I was feeling all weird that day previous to hearing the news about the tickets that I believe I already explained the confusions with the last night escapade of outstanding bliss but also left with a bit of confusion of what I was intended to do with myself if I was expected to do anything really. I don't really think anyone expects anything honestly though you just expect things of yourself and you don't ask questions unless you are put into a situation where someone is demanding something to happen and those situations are why I think some people are so miserable or the world. There is no time to think in this capitalist society and those who do think waste allot of time doing that and can't get paid. I am lucky I can pay for things. Don't have to worry about housing really that's all paid for by my parents but I still feel trapped like I can never make enough to live on my own. It seems like it would be easier to wander around homeless almost or like it could be more enjoyable thinking about supporting your castle and clones day in and out and you have no time to think except maybe when you would watch the news when you get home and that is bias propaganda; you can try looking through the lines but that takes dedication. I have time to read books and that almost seems all I have time to do I can't collect my thoughts so well or collaborate with others most people around where I live are turned off by all the political talk. It is surprising to see how many I can find that agree with me however, more people are more liberal than I expect. Most people at my workplace seem to be democrats' at the most conservative extent and, makes me think the only conservatives that have got to be around are the stereotypical rich guy archetype. They are too controlled we all are and told to pursue pleasure and this pursuit of happiness but monetary goods are so limited and almost seems like the only genuine enjoyment we can receive in all our lives with the rapidity of it all. If I stop and look around most of the time I realize I am not really happy but I put on a show and act and no one wants to talk about real things. I sometimes enjoy nice conversation about things and that's when I feel my best not through action but through voicing concerns and our lives, that is what feels best and most genuine. Then there are the interests the dorky little things that I enjoy and can talk lengths about like music and fiction and it is always a delight to show off my useless knowledge but where were we… about to go to the jazz club that no other person could go. It was just me and Katrina again; we went out to the streets and were off in a taxi so we didn't get lost like last time.

This cab driver was pretty interesting too and as usual Katrina drummed up some conversation out of him; we were talking about sports like basketball and stuff and about how the Green Mill used to be Al Capone's hideout or something. That was pretty interesting we all thought I am pretty sure. He dropped us off across the street from it and I think we split paying for him this time. I had to give something because I felt so bad for not paying for any drinks on our other venture. Katrina almost seemed surprised that I wanted to pay I guess like almost as she took it as I was trying to be some gentleman on a date but it wasn't like that I just wanted to have good time at a jazz club. We crossed the street and on to the Green mill. It cost money to enter; there was a large African American man guarding the entrance into the cocktail lounge from inside. We paid him and went on in there were tons of people already inside; I wished that we would have come a bit earlier because it was all crowded. There were allot of people talking but there was an additional crowded atmosphere that would be real obnoxious if not for the great jazz music layering the air. The band played Latin Jazz music; they made a little joke about singing in Latin because of Americans being all worried about immigrants and he said "We should speak any language we want; it's America right?" Everyone laughed including myself and everyone cheered and the band began to play; Katrina did me a kindness and got me a Vodka with cranberry juice; my signature drink, I guess. It was great not much room to dance or anything but I bobbed my head and swayed to the music's rhythm. I don't know if I could dance like some of the others they like actually were doing "real" dancing like the mambo or something I didn't know any of that. There was one fancy boy rich cat I distinctively remember; he seemed to think he was all that and such a playboy with all the women and stuff but I don't know I think part of my assumptions about his thoughts and what he thought he was were true and the realization of that made me not like him more. I don't know why, I just don't like cocky people and I especially dislike when they don't have allot of room to say it but enough to boast above you. I would never boast about talent if I were specifically talented in anything and what is writing or imagination or art it is something anyone can do, it is what people have to rely on if they were not born into a good status.

Our newly found friends were here and we chatted with them I couldn't hear much anything with all the noise I just nodded my head. We mentioned the art museum is something I remembered and the one guy with all the other girls we met, a guy that looked kinda like Leonardo Dicaprio to be honest tried describing this thing he saw in the gift shop or entrance like this big glass ball thing or something I didn't quite remember it or didn't see it or didn't seem to think it was distinctly that great to remember, it could have been any of those things. Katrina went chatting with someone else she kinda went back between the people there because they had problems with about forming something together when apparently it could be pretty good or something; if that makes sense I didn't know much of what went on but I figured it was something. I talked to Dicaprio a little about how I liked jazz and the first place I heard it was from Frank Zappa not distinctly just jazz but had allot of that in his music and about my brother being in a jazz stage band at my high school and seeing them perform, and I said and I really like to listen to Miles Davis. He said yeah Miles Davis, that is like classic stuff and he talked about how he liked the trumpet as an instrument and yeah I loved that too. I forget where the subject arose but I also mentioned my vegetarianism and we went on about the factory farming and I gave him some news about it that he previously never heard I guess and that was the fact that in addition to the growth hormones they give them hormones that increase how many babies they make at once so they can get the most amount of meat as possible, just all the overproduction it is horrifying to think about. I can't imagine how the workers there can even do it and live with themselves and all that; they must take people who are mentally insane and give them this job. Katrina came back from her cigarette and talking she kinda asked if I had seen anyone like that caught my eye. I honestly wasn't thinking to look and was just confused on what to say really. I blurted out how she was looking nice I didn't really mean it as a kinda weird complement but I also had a sort of underlying thought about it like perhaps she will like me or be open to something. I didn't really want anything I really didn't know. I dread to think what would happen if she took it as something serious; she just maybe thought I was a bit tipsy and had underlying motives and in a way I did but in all honesty didn't if that makes sense. I couldn't really commit and she said that I was sweet and I got all depressed because I was stupid and looked stupid my pride was completely abdicated from my soul I gulped down a big slurp of vodka and got really dazed I was trying to drink my sorrow away and didn't care if I died right then and the jazz music turned somber it was this kinda cool slow jazz that the singer told the people if they had a girl it would be the perfect time to dance with her and all the phony bull shit. I was just real out of it; I went to the restroom and wrote some bullshit "poetry" on the wall "life is a fucking bitch piss and moan and what…" someone came in and I felt silly writing on the wall like a parent telling their child not to write on the wall with crayon and I proceeded to go in for what I meant to do which was piss I suppose I came out still depressed and all that. It was like Katrina was trying to make up for feeling bad but there was nothing she could do I was determined to be just upset and I had more vodka and cranberry juice, she wanted me to dance like before at the House of Blues, I was so fucking happy then, dance, dance, dance, it rang through and I "danced" it was wild I didn't know what I was doing I thought I was dancing with her but all of a sudden I think I switched partners with one of our new found friends and I was trying to imitate what everyone else was doing but I just didn't go to jazz clubs often I guess to "get it". She started laughing and we both laughed and I staggered and the dancing just kinda turned more into ludicrous "bumping and grinding" type of stuff and I staggered more and after that burst of dancing and feeling silly I had to rest for awhile I didn't feel like I was dancing with anyone though I felt like some kinda clown ragdoll being thrown around the place but I was doing it myself in hopes that if I couldn't be smart enough to find a sensual connection with anything someone would take advantage of me and do it for me but no one offered. I wondered where the fuck is all the sluts that people talk about? It didn't seem like the world was so sexual everyone was turned off of it almost or people had higher expectations than I thought even if there were sluts they had more dignity to hang with me and I didn't care I didn't want sympathy but I didn't want to be a monster and plow people like an animal I wanted someone to hold to take me in their arms and whisp me away from everything, I wanted to dissolve into eternity, I wanted to be cared for unconditionally and I wanted them to be happy too I wanted everyone to be happy I didn't feel human I couldn't make a connection with anything was I supposed to have a penis because it didn't feel right sticking into anything but down the toilet where the wastes would enter into all existence into the water the flowing streams forever and ever amen but I don't believe in a god and he can't give me what I need. I don't want to be fucked by a big old man in the sky. I felt like I should be the woman more receiving a seed rather than giving something to someone else and there is being safe but I look at it the same way. I don't see how anyone just has sex for the sake of having it there has to be some connection anyone has to even think it through and that such connection never could be made. Was it religion that hindered my social interactions so much and turned me into this wreck outside of society? God gave up on me but I was sucking god's old penis so long no one wanted to hang around me I was too fucking weird from drinking all of God's semen and then the oceans dry up and the ice melts and his children drown because I drank all his semen and my mouth in not a vagina and where will his children go out of my ass because I don't care about anything I just want a connection and then maybe I can care, why do I need a connection at all why can't I just do things. I guess that's all I'll ever do.

I was brought outside to get some air away from all the commotion and sober me up and the others were all encouraging me saying I am a trooper and this and that but

I didn't feel anything. It made me feel better, they saw I was upset and tried being nice but no one can fully understand me and I can't understand myself because of all the molding that has shaped around me all the things I used to accept and now must relearn. I felt like I learned allot honestly about myself but I don't know how I would help it because I knew now I couldn't get drunk enough to have sex with anyone on my own accord. I would never be that confused, I knew that I shouldn't have sex with anyone and if anything people were to have it with me but no one was really interested. I wasn't a neatly dressed gay man and I was a woman that looked like a man that no man or woman would want anything to do with. I was left alone a little bit I think Katrina bummed a cigarette off of someone and they were real nice and she gave them an overview of what we were doing out here in Chicago and she said Amnesty International and the kids actually knew what she was talking about, I wish I lived in the city allot of these different people that kinda gave a shit about something or were at least knowledgeable about it. I gave some homeless guy two dollars and he thanked me said "God bless" I think and I slurring said don't mention it. Katrina said I didn't need to do what I did and with the same slur I said I wanted to and I don't think it was me drunk I would have anyway I meant that and I didn't know why. Who cares if the guy was going to by booze maybe he was sad, there is too much in this world to not at least want to bring a limited amount of happiness for a moment. I looked into the air for a moment and thought about nothing in particular and said I think I can go back inside now.

We walked back in but instead of vodka I had water on account of how miserably drunk I was. I felt just so sorry about everything all these burdens falling on Katrina's shoulders and at this point I couldn't reverse anything what I said was there my silliness and all the attention it diverted from her good time. Also dealing with the relations among Dicaprio and mystery woman (I forget all our newly found friends' names). I was just sitting drinking my water sitting on a stool looking kinda depressed still and I think others noticed and thought what a loser, what a bum, he won't make it anywhere. Katrina asked about leaving after another in and out of the club. One douche kid complained about us being able to come in without paying little did he know that we had paid previously and the one guy knew that too. I said something indecisive which was common for me in everything when concerning a decision I wanted what others wanted I didn't want to inconvenience anyone. I felt like a prostitute stoned in bible times when I did do something wrong against another because such a high standard was expected of me in particular because I wore a yin yang around my neck and sometimes peace symbols on my shirts. Everyone else had so much fun though and I just couldn't perhaps everyone was better at hiding. I couldn't lie very good. I broke down in the club started crying hoping that I could still be friends and hugged Katrina I gripped her body intensely as if it kept me from falling into some abyss. There was nothing below and nothing above but it seemed so dear to me all the same. It was late and dark and I think and she thought that we should finally go and we departed from the Green Mill. Leaving still with the glad feeling of going to listen to the jazz. The cab driver was all hip again and I was broken up and it was time to get back home.

I was crying all the way there and I kept saying I have to pay you back you did so much and I have been so dumb she kept saying not to worry and said she had fun and all that and it didn't matter to her to pay. The 5th floor awaited us and everyone was still awake to view my ridiculous behavior. I couldn't break out of my rut and stuffed my face with a bagel and it took so much effort to chew. I felt like a child that needed to be taken after and now before me was a book that was my bottle. One of the only things I knew. It wasn't Kafka about alienation that I knew so well but a new author Kerouac.

Jack Kerouac

I began to read it the book On the Road.

> "I first met Dean not long after my wife and I
> split up. I had just gotten a serious illness that
> I won't bother to talk about, except that it had
> something to do with the miserably weary split
> up and my feeling that everything was dead."

I read those words and they pierced my heart like butter and I made silent tears that fell onto the pages. I didn't get after a break because nothing started; Katrina was not my wife and it would just never happen. I have already talked in much detail all about it but if you only saw me in the moment after I would say I had the feeling everything was dead. Everything was very dead to me and I was feeling my life drain for it took much effort for me to read beyond those two sentences without crying it just captured my situation and I felt like I had a friend. I continued reading and Jack wrote before Sal met Dean he always dreamed of going out west and "on the road" and how he vaguely planned but never took off. I had the same feeling all the time at my rural house in which I lived just going out "on the road" but I never took off until I kinda did in Chicago for this trip and in many ways I paralleled Sal's trip on the road to me visiting Chicago.

They introduced the characters I remember thinking Katrina was like Dean because he seemed to have more experience being out on the road and all but he was all interested in sex and I didn't think that was where her mind was at and perhaps my mind was there for just but a moment but only in spurts; I felt like all of the characters I guess in a sense I could connect with most of them one way or another especially today or rather tonight for that is when I read it.

I read this section about Dean and instantly thought of flashbacks when I pretended to listen to all the talk of people when Jack typed out how Dean was like a young boxer in the corner when you spoke to him always looking down nodding his head back and forth to make you think he was listening to every word saying things like yes a thousand times and that's right. I did similar things within talking confusion with my drunken daze when I wanted to keep someone talking when I didn't feel like talking or feel I had not much to add to a conversation I would do the same routine nodding the head saying yes, yes, yes and all that. Sal in the book was a writer and Dean wanted to show him how to write I wasn't showing anyone and hell I don't know if I could teach it; it is just a thing that flows out of you and out of your mind and this is how I connected to the Sal character, the fact he was a writer and having the vague plans about traveling but never committing till he ventured with friends. And then there was Carlo Marx. This seemed to be a joke on the character represented in the book that I believed was to be Allan Ginsberg but Carlo was a man familiar with all the jargon of intellectuals like Karl Marx and I liked to think I was familiar with the man like my pal Carlo in the novel.

Carlo was described as the mind and a poetic mind too and Dean was the con man. I didn't relate with the con man side or perhaps I did to an extent letting on that I knew more than I did or pretended to be someone like Carlo at times maybe I was conning people that way I don't think I fooled anyone but I never really contented myself on my mind and the things I said I wanted to sound smarter than I did though I guess to some people I must have sounded like Karl Marx or Noam Chomsky or something. I remember people being impressed with my jargon and talk at work and stuff. My mother said I was a smart boy but misguided and yadaydayada. It seemed like the Breakfast Club movie no one could just be one person from it they were all of them and all that. I was a bit of Sal, Dean and Carlo all rolled into one and I didn't have an abundance of any of these things but enough to feel connected to their characters. I was a writer longing for experiences, pretended to listen and know things and a little bit of me "knew" things. My intellectualness was unique and genuine for the most part I kept myself well read and liked to spout it off when I remembered a good bit of something or thought it could relate to something and tried to make it connect to lots of different things. I didn't say I was some intellectual but liked to practice what I knew in order to feel more like one.

Carlo acted deep and tried sounding serious with all he said and part of me thought all this political stuff was all a joke but I also thought if it is what is there to live for it must be important or something must be important if we acted like nothing was important we would all go mad or were we mad to obsess over things. Something about Dean struck me as Bukowskian but very different in another aspect. Bukowski seemed to think in a Nietzschean sort of frame only he made hopelessness sound funny and didn't see much meaning in life. Dean struck me as a character who in spite of all that hopelessness wanted to live life and Bukowski seemed determined not to live because doing things for nothing was too much effort and Dean doing things for the sake of doing them was the only way to live to do things with all the surprises down the road to truly live. Carlo lived through his books and his Karl Marx and all that liked to talk it and Sal wrote thing down. Sal wasn't a political person like Carlo and became increasingly more like Dean and accepted a style of living for experience and he would write about his experiences but it would not continue as Sal but as someone else in another one of Jack's tales and there was a character very much like Dean who lived thoroughly by living but perhaps with more noble cause or intent like in the Dharma Bums, a book I would later read was Japhy who devoted so much into Buddhism; he just lived it and lived life to its fullest when the guy put his mind to something he would just do it but that's a whole other time and period of myself my life this is for the here and now and all I heard was Dean's lifestyle of sensual living and empiricist delight.

This book was so essential to my growth in this weekend; it told me to not take life so seriously and to take things as they come. I would think to do some major changes in my life take more risks and with the first real chance I had I would go out on the road again. I needed more experiences I wasn't living enough. They knew an awful lot through literature and I thought about things allot and allot about what I read, I wrote the thoughts down but long have I waited to actually live and what great interest it would be to get more experience into my writings I thought, what great joy, how helpful it could all be I thought.

This book helped me cope with all that happened for some reason. It just seemed to mean everything in the moment I picked it up that night all that commotion and ridiculousness that happened. Jack Kerouac was like my savior in this moment and there was no Jesus Christ there never seemed to be for me, he died and never came back and that was a long time ago. Kerouac died but he never claimed to be back again or maybe being a Buddhist or focusing on it later he came back as someone else in another life or perhaps he found Nirvana who knows. All I know is most words I read in this brief moment of my life meant allot and I forget how many chapters I read before I was too tired and "hit the sack" as they say. I eventually did and the feeling rose a bit the next day as I read more but it was less potent then. Funny how feelings rise and fall maybe we are all in the same motion but it is just something we do to ourselves to feel in step with others like we only react to situations to pretend things affect us a such and such a way. I felt this pressuring of society sometimes like I would be caught with this lack of desire for something but people just wanted you to react and be some way. It kinda felt like me being here at this conference in a sense I was very serious like Carlo but didn't give a damn also like Dean. It was all some dilemma but wasn't really one at all in another sense it just was. I would be forced to deal with it and that is no big thing; it's not a trap it's life and that's something that's there and isn't the greatest moments are what you don't expect and you get those by exploring things. You can do it anyway you please writing, thinking, reading, living and I suppose even not living is a method just doing the same thing day in and out expecting some god above to change it. Perhaps things will change and perhaps they won't you usually can tell how much depending on where you exist in the moment of things. I have seen prisoners free through Amnesty and people not watching can miss that maybe they just expect activists to be active and "change" things and perhaps I have done things in much the same vein. I could do more but don't do too much because I want to be comfortable but what have I to lose. Happiness and freedom is all just someone relative; it's what you make it, it's where your heart lies. If you are content being a lazy blob watching television and indulging in other joys of a common proletariat and complaining about not being able to suck more of the bourgeoisie's tit than you can live that way, you can take life as a working proletariat who is devoted to changing the way you see things and the way they seem determined to stay but you have to suck someone's tit I suppose. It is your ideas that you must feed, you must constantly say yes this is important and nothing can tell me otherwise compromise will haunt my success, what will happen if I try too hard? Will I be unmade and made captive and killed like in 1984 or similar works? Is it fiction or reality it is reality if you let it be and this and that? Things are what you make them you are only as trapped as you want to become.

CHAPTER 12

Voting Day and Some Other Things

The next day was a day when we all experienced the city together and it was also Election Day for Amnesty International members. We all gathered in a room and did our voting. The issues concerning focusing on the rights of children to have rights to medication despite parental religion nuts and obviously everyone was concerned about such an issue and that it must be pursued just like all human rights issues. There were other issues both of which I can't remember unfortunately or perhaps it wasn't too unfortunate because it would not have been so interesting for it wasn't so quick to my memory; I asked my friends if they remembered anything and that was in vain for they didn't remember it must have been forgettable I suppose one thing I did remember however was the ridiculous democratic ways of the people at this voting session. They brought up minor points that hardly made a difference whilst being changed something's I believed were left better unchanged based on their phrasing previously as opposed to the new but there were changes I enjoyed and I liked the fact that people were willing to argue points even if they were quite silly and perhaps even petty it showed these people were involved. I was a bit let down previously when I heard how the group leaders didn't want to hear from members too much or discouraged their insight but this time they were pretty much made to listen and acknowledge it would be very democratic otherwise and it ironically wouldn't be very human rights when it was after all a human rights organization. I remember this woman who always seemed to have something to say she was from some Middle Eastern country and brought up the atrocities that happen on account of U.S. intrusion. She seemed angry and passionate about it and existence damn anyone who says she doesn't know what she is talking about she lived there she experienced it all; she received much applause because most people at Amnesty were well aware of these things but then I thought here we are sitting in this room listening to these people I suppose everyone from our group including myself and people from other groups should have been trying to organize with each other and make a difference or something you all that cliché rubbish. Making a difference what difference can anyone make when they have a state that they listen to? If there is a state we need to shape it for the benefit of education not blind obedience and all these things movies, cheap food, bottled water, soft drinks, anything with a label yeah that will shorten time. Why does time need to be shortened? Why don't I just go on and rabble about everything under the sun. different time different place but time is different depending where you live and where you are and what is time irrelative, irrelevant just a function to decide when these people need to clock in clock out working for the clampdown ha gitalong gitalong gotta work to live and live to work that is the only thing we can do and we got a good thing going we can relax and enjoy our idiot box and our video games and even a book once in a while as long as it's just for entertainment and you don't take much of it to heart, fine take it to heart but I would like to see you put it to practice it never works can't you see how bad things are, and at the same time they are so well, you should be content don't be sad just live but not too much don't think about things and if you do just think and perhaps you can write them down you can even make a buck maybe on it but for the love of our Christian god don't do anything for God's sake don't do anything based on these ideas from the evil thinking liberal intellectual men and women no not those feminist whores that are anything but but we won't tell you that we just say they wish they were a slut and they don't have the goods you gotta cash it in you should get more go to the clouds grab the flame like Prometheus but expect to get burned if you don't support our way of life unless you don't threaten the other god's up in mt. Olympus. Isn't it more just to help the many then the few you ask but there is different class? What makes that important I work for a living. What is work and what's the importance? To be a productive member of society and some cliché shit like that. I don't want to support this society or any "society" unless it is a society labeled humanity... I have touched off base. What determines what is right or wrong anyway. I think as I type and pressing the keys I think what meaning does it all have these strange inscriptions that we all recognize so well flail across my computer screen and they are there. They exist they existed in my head and perhaps they exist in some form of ideal if there are maxims to live by or whatever. We have to make our own how do we know we are right well that's just it we don't but the you can try and you can't try and both situations you are helpless to be free human rights becomes a strange phrase with such existential thoughts for what rights can we not have? We are hopelessly free until a god is formed or a state is formed and still then we allow ourselves to suck on the teat and to be dependent on it even as old men and women and we contract some horrible disease from this milk that has gone so bad it always was bad. Idealism is a weird thing; it almost seems inevitability as soon as you place something into the present in a flash it turns to the past. Action is what counts action with a decent mind and minds must be made indecent by following certain forms of idealism so closely in a way everything is idealism what can we base of material and this materialism lifestyle things exist we put them into being we give them names we are our own gods. God did not invent forks as they were as people made. Were men meant to use utensils? To ask the religious person did God just invent humans to watch them invent things and act as gods themselves and see an inevitable collapse when a few individuals thought they should indulge in things and the poor don't matter so much they don't know better they are lower primates and it is social Darwinism, the religion of the Capitalist but things aren't based so much on merit these objects that make money are made for their use they are made in abundance and people don't need it. The television tells them they do and they buy it in the supermarkets that impoverished kids across the world slave to make such things out of cheap plastic so they can't be paid too much. What determines worth? How good it looks? A dollar isn't so nice to look at. Was Ben Franklin one of the highest bills because he was a ladies man is sex the measure of worth? If precious luxuries are lower than sex then why pay so much into green paper and more green papers so you can have a building all for you that look just so very nice why you want it to look so good and so well. It is a part of your image if you have nice things I guess you are a nice person. You appear decent for you have no reason to be perturbed for you don't live in despotism, you are not thrown away when you get what you have, and you are secure.

That man on the street I think about people mock him say oh he will just get booze but it is all he knows and frankly all he is allowed. They will say he is an alcoholic and he can't fight it unless he believes in higher powers be it wealth, government, god or whatever. He pays to be at seminars to make people help him through it they make money through his suffering and he isn't enjoying himself he is probably there sitting there saying how terrible this problem and deprive himself of the thing that gives him joy if only for a limited time. I don't think he would have these troubles with a secure home or a good school around his area when he was younger so he could learn to be something or do something more than be a consumer and another mass of suffering people abroad. He makes our lives miserable we are doing all we can to support his lazy sorry ass; he is selfish his relatives say or probably say. What is your crutch why is it a problem for you and they are probably struggling to with their home and everything and there is this guy coming to the door asking for the money. Do they give him support? I don't know I am making a hypothetical situation but perhaps instead of relying on the almighty dollar to solve his problems perhaps take time to invite him in your home help him with whatever hang ups he has. Perhaps you could learn from it yourself. The individual is praised in America in capitalism not community everything is too hectic gotta look out for me when I can but our enemy shouldn't be each other but the people so many say are the supplier of this stuff we can get; like gods dropping manna from the heavens we receive the scraps while they dine on the sacrificed animals forbidden to be eaten by those unworthy but again who is worthy.

Well anyway the voting concluded with some changes which were a pick me up I suppose it showed these leaders were at least mildly supportive of its members I suppose like a state socialist system. I would probably be satisfied with that as a final political system I just don't want to hear about poverty and suffering. This can't be done simply burning books people thrive on explaining and knowledge and trying to understand things but are told it's inevitable this is the way things are and the only way they can be. I don't care about liberty as far as people suffer less. I think suffering ultimately disintegrates through liberty if I am wrong locking me up. I don't know allot but I read I don't live or at least haven't done much living; this trip I suppose was a slice of life. I didn't worry about supporting myself and didn't spend my whole time indulging in material possessions, I talked to people and listened and learned to things people said and had an overall good time with my comrades and what else really can be asked for?

It was finally time to head for home but we all wanted to see some of the city. Some people wanted to visit the field museum and we also had to have some Chicago pizza. I forget what we did first but I have to say I don't think I've had anything quite like Chicago pizza; I have had imitations in Ohio pizza shops and no it is not Chicago pizza. All the cheese was under the tomato sauce and the toppings were all underneath and it was just so big and filling one slice would be enough really. As I said we also went to the field museum; we couldn't really stay too long but we glimpsed at all these taxidermy sculptures of animals. I have always loved animals, ever since I was a child and I would read books about animals. I always gravitated to what was unique and now that I think about it animals people didn't like typically. The creepy crawly things like lizards, snakes, bats and strange insects. Maybe it was just to be different. I think I liked the darker more mysterious things though. I always enjoyed Bible stories with all that magic stuff in them because it was so mystifying like reading about superhuman people in comics but apparently this was real life; I found out that most religion was probably phony though and the magic was gone but I suppose I found more in something that isn't superficial something even more unknown. Maybe science fiction wasn't so fictitious and perhaps there were other worlds out there with their own supermen and so on. I hoped for that because earth has gotten so boring maybe we were getting so sick of it we were unconsciously trying to destroy it. We say an exhibit about the forests of the world and what people were doing and all that depressing stuff. There was this interesting interactive thing I forget if it was connected with the exhibit but there were floating balls on a monitor and you could keep them up by an image of yourself projected upon the screen. I stood there and tried keeping things up and Kate was playing this game too she was more successful at it. I ended up with only one ball left partially because I was trying to send some of the other balls somewhere and work together with it but now she had them all. I realized something really just symbolic about it all. Trying is an inevitable thing you are going to fall and lose things once and a while but living with what you just do or can do. It's like things have a way of working themselves out and things are bad and they are good and it's like karma I guess. Perhaps I made too much about this observation of a simple little activity but it seemed to mean allot but I put meaning to it based on all these crowded thoughts I have been thinking.

I recollect an Egyptian exhibit and remember a man ranting about how the Bible got much of the Egyptian history wrong and he was apparently an expert and this and that I don't know why this seems valid to bring up. Religion is a thing that has irked me; I pretended not to know it or think it but it just told you to not enjoy things but then again it told you to be content with all things and thinking now how unhuman it seems how unnatural most religion is. It is just making up an explanation for the unexplained. I don't like to bother with metaphysical questions unless I am acting playfully the ideas make for good story ideas I suppose but that is just it. Metaphysical things are for tales to read to enjoy and things go awry you delude your mind and think these things are truth and they are worse when we create consequences for disobeying these structures of the mind and the imagination. We left the field museum and I wished we could stay to really look at the evolutionary section so that I may be able to explain those ideas to religious people when they ask about the world. I think the big bang theory is hog wash or just them giving up on theories of the world though. I don't know if it was a bang or chemicals spontaneously occurring or perhaps it was always there and is ever expanding but we don't know the beginning. We are the beginning we exist. We are ourselves and that is all that warrants our thinking as far as beginnings are concerned. We are just here and we are going to have to deal with it and make the best of it. It is not a struggle and at the same time it is because of the nauseating inevitability of everything. You can look at it in two lights positive and negative and that is relative to you. You consciously chose pessimism as much as optimism in most cases. There are thinkers, accepters and consumers. I suppose there are variations of the three. There are thinkers who live to produce these things to consume, thinkers to resist the oppression of what being content leads those led astray by producing thinkers. The accepters must not think and only consume or if they think there must be no action being done and not much whispering or bantering, most of the time they don't think of it. The accepters consume as well as the thinkers. Most people consume however but that is through the fact that most people garner some acceptance within them. The wealthy thinkers or consumers buy the big houses and nice cars to show everyone they have money. The other thinkers mostly will buy books to learn more about these systems and they will look for the least possible way to get these books and education materials without supporting the system and food of course must be bought and any other necessity that seems relevant to have; they live according to need and their entertainment their leisure is devoted to education or activism or something such as that. The poor consumers are like the poor alcoholic man that may not have been an alcoholic again it was a hypothetic analogy to explain some things on my mind. After all of this we traveled our way on back to Ohio.

CHAPTER 13

This Is A Long Drive For Nothing To Think About

And then we were on our way back home and we didn't really talk about much. I didn't even think about all that much to tell the truth... Ironically we put in another cd labeled This Is A Long Drive For Nothing To Think About by the band Modest Mouse. Not many people have heard of them or perhaps you could say many have but I don't know if there are too many fans. I am a fan and there was at least one other fan in the vehicle. Everyone complained about the second track though which I didn't quite understand but I was pretty fine with it. We continued driving as we listened to the singing of Isaac Brock and performing instruments of the band members who manipulated them to make the right sounds or the wrong sounds depending on you taste I guess. We were pretty much on a long trek for home I don't remember much of what anyone talked about at that moment pretty much the only thing on my mind was that I would be leaving my friends and would have to live with my mostly Christian family and that irked me and I would work at my thankless job stocking shelves made by basically slave labor most likely, it amazes me how I can keep from being sick as I place these things on the shelf. I have brief moments where I think upon it and then I think what can I do what can I fucking do about it and fuck it never mind. I felt like I must devote to something but at the same time I didn't really but regardless I felt for encouraged to partake in this seemingly endless journey to have the world recognize the rights of all. It seems so simple that people should recognize this but somehow it has become utopian. A sociologist Max Weber had a theory of Christianity and capitalism being connected. They went against the catholic church because they didn't like the debt they had to pay for their services and in Protestantism everyone was their own priest but for some reason they still dwelled on the guidance of the preacher and of the dogma. They didn't do the religious practices of Catholics and couldn't figure out a way to imprison its followers to it so they said God blessed his followers through their wealth and gain on earth. Apparently they thought if you followed some abstract nonsense of a deity watching over you; God would throw you a bone. It is likely slightly intelligent people started realizing god wasn't Santa Claus so they had to earn their respect and get all the money they could and the wealthy now choose who goes to heaven and not god for making it harder for the people that they don't like to gain wealth. I didn't want to buy into it I hated Christians but especially the Protestants for their capitalistic sensibilities.

I didn't think about all that on the car ride back to Ohio but then again it's something usually always on my mind. It rings in my head and I can't think of how to stop it. I can't think it away that is just it; there needs to be action I need to "do" and that is what I am trying to determine myself to do. The world is too lifeless the world needs passion and I don't see it on a daily basis only in spurts with my activist group, in my head and in the pages of the books I read. The songs I listen to there is passion, not on main stream air waves it's just lifeless meaningless dribble. I feel that I should determine to change it because it is so much better when music has a purpose. I am a musician but I am distracted by the books I read but the books I read are determined to give me inspiration, it is the same with my writings. I also must apparently have time to enjoy myself have fun and be a normal young person to not turn so many heads. They will tear off your head but everything has a price and I suppose the more meaningful the larger the cost no one gives their life to something if they believe it has no value the things they do. People are told when they vote their vote matters but think if citizens were at least a little bit active in pursuing the polices and the way the system works what our nation does to other countries to "promote democracy" while it is actually deterred abroad. I am just one person I rant and rave on social networking sites, I raise my voice whenever I feel a subject seems the least bit convenient to add my political insight to the conversation, I am writing this novel in hopes some people might think about these things I have been discussing the things talked about on the trip.

We stopped at a gas station another BP. Melissa hated getting gas there she rather would get it at Sunoco for reasons of slightly more ethical practice. There didn't seem to be as many Sunoco's greed pays off I guess. The cheaper the labor, the less safety measures made for proper handling of materials, the less eco friendly, the more it pays the rich fat cat owning the company for the most part. Am I correct in wanting to follow this path of goodness when in America it seems the slogan is cheat if you can't win push and shove to get ahead it's all about you. The Nietzsche creed the "will to power" resonates within my mind I want to reject it but then I see situations of the past in Central America where Nicaragua tried giving social services to their citizens with a more free government than the Somoza dictatorship supported by the U.S. only to have the U.S. and Iran paid Contras to slaughter and destroy the products of wealth used on health education that they could have spent on defense but they were "too kind". Damn I remember a time my pastor's wife used the phrase to define president Jimmy Carter, a pastor's wife I thought, how could she say anything could be "too nice" she seemed a nice enough person but how is it fucking wrong to be too nice does god not want us to be too nice she must know she's married to a pastor, apparently they are supposed to have a link to god but alas I hang my head down in knowing people can only guess god's will or rather they create it. I can't believe in "will to power" for who likes suffering there must be suffering when people "will" over others and exploit them. No one likes to suffer regardless of their definition of such things.

Outside getting gas and waiting for the others the others were all but Katrina and myself again for some reason it seemed we always happened to be ended up with each other. I told her again about being sorry but she said she had fun and I had fun and then I didn't know why I was apologizing. She asked about like what I thought about my whole sexuality and I decided I was transgender once and for all. This seemed so imprisoning though and I thought it unfair I can't have romantic relations with like anyone. I needed to look like a woman to feel comfortable with one in the same way a heterosexual man would a woman. I just didn't feel I wanted to grow through all of it now; it seemed I would have to wait too long to have enough money to go through a change. It's the price I have pay from god which is society or the state for there is no difference if one is to speak of god. So much judgement and you can scream oh just fuck them they don't know me all you want but the voices don't fucking stop. They will still whisper perhaps glare if they know the truth. The labels the gender labels are what kills me rather than my birth right. I have to be as a man I must look at myself as such and must be identified by all of society as one and that is what irks me I just want to be a human but I feel like an alien that doesn't below I feel like an animal that can grip with "reality" whatever they claim that is. I could barely talk to Katrina at this moment I hated getting chocked up I couldn't help letting it out though I held it in so long to keep the image up it just comes out consistently. I just ended up being at a loss of most words for the most part because it felt like I might die if I said how I felt and I didn't want to die despite my misery it didn't seem like it would make much difference somehow I felt I would feel it in my death was it an instilled fear of hell, was it a devotion to humanity, why do people fight to protect their bodies at most every cost and what wills someone to take their own life. It's a question that will haunt me until my day of death or perhaps we never die we just go to something else and we become part of the world or even go into another realm however I think the first two are more likely somehow. Maybe when the our world ceases to sustain itself new life will grow from it and start anew maybe someone from far away will visit and wonder if anyone had ever been to earth if any remnants of that title exist anymore after it is all over if we allow things to end. That should be the goal to experience and learn as much as we can about the universe and everything.

I think I was encouraged to take more chances I realized after two days after the trip my mouth was rather active in my school classes. I could swear that I encouraged most of the students in my philosophy class to think more anarchistic or socialistically or basically question capitalism right to have the crown as the self-proclaimed god of political systems. I was so encouraged by this and I continue to be more active in my postings about things I learn from books onto social networking sites some thought it was interesting some wanted to argue and others were bothered by it but at least it might get some people thinking and that is all I intend to do. My facebook status was changed from male to transgender female and I continued living out my transgender lifestyle to take away much of the masculine qualities of my appearance I shaved more often including my arms, chest and legs on occasion. I felt better but it wasn't enough I was still abit too worried about judgment I suppose.

We didn't listen to Modest Mouse all the way we opted out for some of the music on James's mp3 player and he had some good metal music that we all listened to and enjoyed. We got back to the school and we said goodbye and I gave everyone a hug my dad probably saw it and said oh good; he has a girlfriend now he manned up and finally is going after some pussy and whatnot he would say it more conservatively but it is what he wanted it's what he meant. The surprise that would await him later. I laugh thinking of the moment he finds out for sure. I felt more like family with my comrades than the people I would soon visit in my own home. I realized that the connections people have with families are coincidental it is only what we make it. The more experiences you share the more intimate the experiences reinforce what your relationships are not your birthright. I felt no special duty to anyone but existence, humanity, and the universe. I don't know if it sounds like a lot of fluff and fake to those who may be reading. If I am to have any devotion it is to these things. I await the new experiences that will be in my life. I can't wait to get "on the road" again. I wanted to start living. I wanted to be like Dean Moriarty and go out into the world and if not taking part in activism exploring myself more deeply and not only behind the cover of books.

I was back into not living within time and living life in a similar way I had before and I keep hoping deep down I could live life like I had in the House of Blues, the Green Mill or the streets of Chicago the way I had with friends by my side and perhaps we would be fighting for some struggle or simply having a good time together either way it was worth anything but going into work and working for the clampdown walking in like a robot hardly memorizing the lay out of the store like it was a dream and I was born just right their to do the tasks I was appointed to do and I would occasionally think of starving children and then I talked about the desperation that we have caused some listened with broken ears ready to listen for the sake of listening and to be respectful and others would like to listen while not fully accepting these views but would be open at least to some of my speech and others liked to chime in and add to my ranting and talk about things they knew themselves obviously I thought they didn't live from around here and I must go again on the road and find these people.

I have read so many things that question existence and life itself where I start to question anything is really there at brief moments and then it falls when someone brings me into their illusions or perhaps it is reality but everything feels empty and unreal to me. People are no more than boards and chairs. The thinking is the difference and what makes something as it is should be nurtured not neutered. People are living things and thinking things and the only way to live a life of worth is to practice our functions not stick to dogmas or routines. I found this upon our trip. As soon as I came back from the trip and before then I was plotting on creating a novel recollecting the experience. I don't know what more to say except that the trip was over but will not end… Blank thoughts not thinking just writing and the sun sets and then we rest but some stay awake and I wonder if they think about those who sleep and then we fade the images of the living fade all day for we can only grip the past with such abstract thought only in an abstract sense can we even acknowledge such a thing but there it is we write it down and life goes on. I could say on and on make it new live anew and keep on living and it would never sink in that is because you already do it and we chose how the time is spent and we follow the traditions and dogmas placed upon us. Is it for us to ashere to this should we explore ourselves, others, the earth, animals, just walk until we find something of sudden interest. Who knows all of us know but it is for us to act we have to do things and it is a circle of the absurd ranting of an amateur and he presses keys type type type and what is it what are we doing what am I doing itch itch

I had an itch on my arm and what does it mean to writing only that the recording of the moment was all down for you to read about. What does it mean to itch what does it matter nothing but it seems that I must end this end all of it this train of words that must eventually come to and end and it doesn't seem to ever find an appealing set of words that would end it so plainly to say here we go let us move on. I will end it with the origin of most things with a verb that brought you here. Fuck… The End?

APOLOGIES

I don't know if you enjoyed this but it is pretty amateur throughout most I believe. It is a person venting grieving and is very much writings in one's journal set to novel form and it is an amateurs two cents about matters. I hope you liked it and I hope I can look back on it and like it but whatever. I don't care if anything is liked or disliked. It is a shot in the dark like anything like life like thoughts like all acts we commit to. A final goodbye and thanks to those who made this novel possible the friends that helped me live through this excursion. I pray to nothing but hope and myself that I may live more experiences like it.